FORMIDABLE
ENEMY

FORMIDABLE
ENEMY

TERRY BRAMLETT

Five Star • Waterville, Maine

First Edition, Second Printing

Published in 2005 in conjunction with
Tekno Books and Ed Gorman.

Set in 11 pt. Plantin.

Printed in the United States on permanent paper.

Library of Congress Cataloging-in-Publication Data

Bramlett, Terry.
    Formidable enemy / by Terry Bramlett.—1st ed.
        p. cm.
    ISBN 1-59414-280-7 (hc : alk. paper)
    I. Title.
PS3602.R3448F67 2005
    813'.6—dc22
                                                        2005004992

Always
for
Brenda

ACKNOWLEDGEMENTS

Writing a novel is an individual process, but producing a book takes a number of people. I'd first like to thank Martin Greenberg and John Helfers for taking a chance on an unknown quantity. Patricia Estrada, my editor, was invaluable in her advice, which made this novel a much better book. My writer's group (Richard Parks, Mark Hoover, Shelley Powers, Grant Kruger, and Heather Clair) helped my writing to improve tenfold between the first draft of *Formidable Enemy* and the final product. Lastly, I have to acknowledge Cecil Bramlett who told me science fiction stories when I was young, instilling a love for wonder and words.

PART ONE

DINGO
THE
MEETING

PROLOG

*From the unedited transcripts of the Court-martial
of Captain Roger Stimson—Closed sessions:*

General Bankston: General Boudreau. When Captain
Stimson released the virus, what was the ultimate effect on the Enochian/Human War?

General Boudreau: I'm not sure what you mean,
Bankston. Stimson released that weapon without direct authorization from me. He disobeyed orders.

General Bankston: Didn't the aliens immediately leave
Earth? The War ended with our victory, due to the
actions of Captain Stimson; is that not correct?

General Boudreau: He did not follow proper military pro-
cedure in the release of the biological weapon. This
tribunal has no choice but to continue.

(Whispering and murmurs in the background.)

General Bankston: The President is getting ready to
honor this man that you wish to court-martial. The
public is in an uproar that this tribunal is considering
any disciplinary action against Captain Stimson. You
certainly see the political and public relations disas-
ters that could come from our continued action in
this case. You are running for political office yourself,
are you not? *(Boudreau nods.)* Tomorrow, this court
will rule that Captain Roger Stimson is acquitted on
all charges.

General Boudreau: Bankston, you must be joking.

11

General Bankston: Rafe, if you want to win your Senate campaign, you had better get on the Stimson bandwagon. Those fools in Congress tried to brand him as a war criminal and the public turned on them. The Army will have no part of this. Roger Stimson cannot be convicted. We must protect the integrity of the military. Stimson broke a number of military laws, but all the public sees is that he single-handedly ended the War. Those damn blue alien bastards ran away so fast that they left thousands behind.

General Boudreau: General Bankston, I must protest. (*Man in suit behind Boudreau whispers in his ear. Boudreau sighs.*) I withdraw my protest, General Bankston, on the advice of my aides.

General Bankston: Thank you, General Boudreau, and good luck on your election. We need men like you in the Senate.

1

Downtown New Orleans cooperated as I cruised through the last day of my seven-day night shift in the Memorial Hospital Emergency Room. Three boys tried to ruin my night by getting shot. They said someone just drove up and began shooting. The bullets passed through fleshy tissue. Two boys were hit in the leg and one in the right buttock, which showed that he had enough sense to run. We sent the gunshot wounds home with a Betadine dressing, telling them to take acetaminophen for the pain.

By three o'clock, we only had one patient in the ER, an LOL (little old lady) who came in because she had not had a bowel movement in two days. I knocked on the door to her room.

"Mrs. Winter? Good morning, I'm Roger Stimson and I'm going to be your nurse this morning," I said with my best empathetic smile. Mrs. Winter looked me over carefully to see if I would be an appropriate nurse for her condition. She opened her mouth to speak, but I spoke first. "Now, what seems to be the problem today?"

"I think I have the constipation," she said.

Good, I thought, *at least she got right to the point.*

She pointed to the lower left side of her abdomen. "I've been paining right there for the last two hours. It woke me up."

I nodded, deciding that she had gas pains, and let it go at that. *This wasn't going to be too bad*, I thought, as I asked for her medical history and other pertinent information. When

13

I finished the history, I told her that the doctor would be with her in a few minutes, that we would be running some tests, and left quickly. She was a nice LOL, but nice LOLs were usually lonely old ladies and talked your ears off, if they thought they had a captive audience. I decided that I would spend some time with her after Dr. Richards finished his assessment.

I walked back to the nurse's station, where Dr. Richards, two other RNs, an ER tech, and the unit secretary were playing a game of hangman. Richards was at the board, proclaiming the phrase represented a movie, but he stopped the game when I sat down.

"Whatcha got, Roger?"

I shrugged. "Little old lady having gas pains who may or may not be constipated," I said, plopping into a chair. "She's probably in more need of the blue-hair special than anything medical."

"Lonely?" Richards crossed his arms and placed the tip of the pen he held against the tip of his nose. He looked down his nose and removed the pen, revealing a black dot. He rubbed at the ink.

"Yeah," I said, trying not to laugh. "Her husband died about two years ago and both her kids live in Dallas. This is her fifth ER visit in the last seven months. I'll bet it's for the same complaint."

The unit secretary said she would go get the file. Dr. Richards went back to the game with the remnant of a black dot on his nose. I wrote my initial assessment. As I charted the LOL, Larry Jones, the ER tech, sat next to me.

"Need any blood?" he asked, hoping for something to do. Larry, new to the ER, didn't know that on the slow nights, you rested up for the nights that New Orleans would kick your ass. I assumed I might have looked like Larry many years ago, with his gaunt face and young, fresh eyes. Experience wore the glitter off the excitement, but for Larry everything was new. I knew my answer would disappoint him. "Wait for Dr. Richards to see her. You may get to give her an enema, but I doubt it."

Larry sighed and looked dejected. "It's too quiet around here," he said, frowning. I heard a groan from Shirley, one of the other RNs. She grimaced and opened her mouth, but stopped when I shook my head.

"Don't kill him, Shirl," I said. "He doesn't know any better. He's new."

Shirley nodded and turned to Larry. "Don't ever, ever say that it is quiet in the emergency room," she said, her voice raspy from twenty years of smoking. "Next time, Roger won't save you."

I agreed with Shirley and returned to my charting. Larry apologized, but looked a little confused. ER nurses acquired more superstitions than a New Orleans Voodoo priestess. Before I could explain to Larry, the radio commanded our attention.

"MEU 235 to Memorial ER."

Shirley groaned and glared at Larry. "Go answer it. It's your fault."

I laughed at Larry's anguished expression. He'd broken the ultimate ER taboo, complaining about a quiet night, but he didn't understand. The gods of nursing would make us pay for his rookie mistake.

Larry walked like a condemned man toward the receiver, scratching his head. "This is Memorial, go ahead," Larry said as he keyed the microphone.

"Memorial, this is MEU 235, Paramedic Stovall reporting. We are en route to your facility with a . . ." The transmission trailed off.

15

I stopped writing and looked up.

"MEU 235, you broke up," Larry said. "Continue your report." He loved talking on the radio to the paramedics. The redness of his face told me that the adrenaline was already pumping.

"That's the problem," the paramedic said in response. "I'm not real sure how to report this." He hesitated, but the radio did not break contact. Larry looked at me. I shrugged.

The paramedic continued. "We have a five-minute ETA to your facility. I don't think this is an emergency patient, but I can't be sure. Patient is obviously inebriated and has a small cut—I guess it's a cut—over his . . . forehead?" The last word sounded more like a question than a statement.

"Get some vital signs, Larry," I said. I've heard paramedics excited and scared, but never confused about anatomy. *This can't be good,* I thought.

"You got vital signs on this patient?" Larry asked.

There was a definite hesitation on the part of the ambulance crew. "I, uh, I wouldn't know where to start. You'll see when we get there. MEU 235 clear." The paramedic shut off the mike and refused to respond to Larry's attempts to re-establish contact.

I looked at Shirley, who was shaking her head. I sighed and said, "This guy, I've got to meet, a paramedic who doesn't know where to start, when taking vital signs." Shirley rolled her eyes.

Since I was charge nurse for the night, Larry asked me where I wanted to put the ambulance patient when he got here. "Put him in trauma room two, just in case."

"Why room two? The paramedic said he didn't think it was an emergency." Larry appeared puzzled.

"There are a couple of reasons for room two," I said. "First of all, the paramedic seemed awfully uncertain, didn't he?" Larry nodded. "Right, so we don't know what we're dealing with. But the major reason is that the medic was sure that the patient was drunk and room two is near the door, so he can leave any time he wants to leave."

"You'd let him leave?" I could see the horror in Larry's eyes. "What if he's really hurt?"

"If he's really hurt, then he'll probably stay until we treat him," I said. "But chances are he's just drunk and will want to sleep it off and leave when he sobers up. Get a suture pack in there for the cut, just in case."

Larry nodded and the horror that a nurse would let a sick person leave the ER faded from his eyes. He needed to understand that we couldn't help someone against his or her will; that's called illegal detainment.

Dr. Richards was with the LOL when the ambulance pulled up. I watched the EMTs unload the patient on the monitor. I didn't like what I saw.

"Damn, his color looks awful," I said to no one in particular. Shirley asked me what I had said. Ignoring her, I ran to room two, yelling at Larry to get Richards into the room, stat. If I was correct, we had a full code on our hands. The patient had looked cyanotic.

I was not correct.

As I entered the room at a controlled gallop, the first thing I noticed was the smell. The stench stopped me dead in my tracks. I knew that smell. *No, it couldn't be,* I thought. *Not in my emergency room.* The EMTs struggled to move the massive patient to the ER stretcher. I couldn't help them because I froze when I saw our new patient's face.

"It's an Enochian," the paramedic said, as he hooked up the oxygen mask to the ER oxygen.

I nodded, noting that neither of the EMTs was old enough to have been involved in the War. The alien's nose smashed against the mask, opening the nostrils wider than normal. Jowls formed at the cheeks and fell on either side of the face. The huge chest heaved forward with each breath, taking the pressure off the nerve-encasing hump I knew the creature possessed on its back. The smell permeated the room, reminding me of garlic and socks worn for a week without washing or airing, which was natural to an otherwise healthy Enochian adult.

The alien's shoulders flowed off the side of the stretcher. His feet hung off, too. He wore extremely large hiking boots. I saw the remnants of denim underneath the sheet covering him. I had forgotten how big Enochians grew. Images of rotting bodies from the old war zone flooded my mind.

The paramedic continued, startling me out of my thoughts. "Now you know why I didn't know how to take this thing's vitals."

I looked at the alien as he lay there, boozed out of his mind. Something bothered me about the alien's treatment. Something so fundamental, I almost forgot. The answer popped into my brain and I laughed. The paramedic turned to me and smiled. I shook my head.

"If you guys don't want to be on the evening news tomorrow, I'd take that oxygen off of him." The paramedic scrunched his eyebrows, not understanding, so I explained. "Our atmosphere has too much oxygen for them, anyway. You're giving him an overdose."

The paramedic ripped the bag off the alien's face. "How was I supposed to know? We didn't study Enochians in school."

I nodded. "I know, and we don't get that many of them in New Orleans. As a matter of fact, I've never seen one here." I bent over and studied the Enochian, who picked that moment to belch. I pulled away, waving my hand in front of my face. I didn't know which was worse, his normal odor or his breath.

The paramedic laughed. "I told you he was drunk." He grabbed a handheld computer off the bed as he chuckled, smiling at me. "You want a report?"

"What the hell is that?" Larry stood at the door with his mouth wide open. I laughed, realizing that I must have looked the same way to the ambulance personnel.

"It's a drunken Enochian," I said. I grinned at Larry. "Wanna draw some blood?"

"Hell no," Larry said, backing away from the door. "I don't want to touch the thing."

"Actually, they're not that bad," I said with a shrug. "Despite the fact they attacked us without warning, most of them were regular people just trying to survive, like you and me."

"People?" Larry stayed at the door. "You've seen these things before?"

I stared at the alien, remembering.

"Oh yeah, you were in the War," Larry said.

I didn't respond. *I have seen way too many of them,* I thought. My mind filled with images of dead, rotting bodies, both human and Enochian, in the Sahara Desert. The stench lingered in my nostrils, after ten long years. Silence covered the carnage as sand burned through my boots. My team collected dead Enochians for research. We had collected quite a few live ones, also for research. I could feel the edges of my guilt pushing to the front of my mind. I tried to shut it out by force of will, but without much success. We kicked the Enochians off Earth, almost annihilating an entire species of intelligent creatures. My research had been a success.

19

When the aliens retreated, I knew that some eleven thousand of them stayed behind, marooned by their race for some reason. The abandoned aliens called themselves the Rejected. The U.S. government gave them a former New Mexico military base to homestead. Giving White Sands to the Enochians seemed the right thing to do, since they already occupied the base. The Enochians preferred hot, dry climates.

"I wonder why this one was in New Orleans." I scratched my head, thinking.

"Hell, if there has to be aliens, they might as well be in the Big Easy," the paramedic said, and punctuated the statement with a laugh, which startled me. I hadn't realized I was talking out loud.

"My mother always said New Orleans is like nowhere else on Earth," Larry said. "The mayor ought to hire this thing to advertise tourism."

The paramedic gave his report. "We picked this thing up underneath an overpass near the old airport. Bystanders said that after the Enochian drank two fifths of Jim Beam, he started yelling that someone was trying to kill the President and somebody had to stop them. One of the onlookers took offense to his tattoo and hit him upside the head with a concrete block."

"Tattoo?" I couldn't picture a tattooed alien. "What color ink do you use for a slightly blue alien?"

The paramedic pulled back the sheet for an answer. I saw the characteristic bulging of what would pass for our pectoralis muscles on the chest. There were no nipples on the blue skin.

But just below where the nipples should have been, a bright red tattoo of an exploding Earth covered the chest. Underneath the Earth was a legend, which read: "EARTH

SUX!" The tattoo artist had added a happy face beside the last word.

"Wow!" Dr. Richards stood at the door. "I haven't seen one of them since the War. He's gotta be drunk. I never saw one that wasn't." Richards walked over to the alien and pulled back the covers. I saw the huge legs that helped the creatures jump over thirty feet, flat-footed. "Nice tattoo."

"Thanks."

Richards took a step back.

The Enochian opened his eyes and looked at the doctor and then around the room at the EMTs, Larry, and myself. "Where the hell am I?" There was no trace of an accent in the perfectly-spoken English.

"You're in the Memorial Hospital ER," I heard myself saying. "Stay on the stretcher until we can determine the nature and severity of your injuries."

The alien emitted a deep, rumbling sound like a semi truck engine at idle, though it was discernible as mirth. His body shook as he laughed, causing the stretcher to sway under the strain. I made a mental note to get a regular bed for the Enochian.

"I can assure you I'm going nowhere at the moment. Two fifths of whiskey will take my body a little longer to metabolize," he said. "I am still quite drunk, thank you." The alien's face skewered into a smile that vanished as quickly as it appeared. He spoke hastily. "What day is it?"

"It's Thursday morning."

He seemed to relax a bit, but asked, "Are you sure?"

When I nodded, I heard him mumble something about five more days. I ignored his babbling. "I need some information for the chart. What's your name?"

The alien started to get up. I wondered how I was going to keep the massive thing in bed long enough to look at that

21

cut on his head, besides checking for damage to the skull from the concrete block. He stood up. I'm six-one and he was at least four inches taller than I, about average height for an Enochian. He seemed unsteady on his feet, so I grabbed his arm. That was my first mistake. He looked into my eyes.

"You've got to help me," he said, almost pleading. I coughed from the smell of whiskey and Enochian phero-mones. "They are going to kill the President and we've got to stop them."

The smell of the whiskey, along with the fear of a mas-sive and possibly psychotic alien, caused me to make my second mistake. I backed away, while he had a death-grip on my arm. I hit the ground first and could see that massive three-hundred-fifty-pound frame falling right on top of me. At the last moment, the Enochian got one leg under him and pushed off, and he flew over my body. I heard the crash as his head went through the wall of ER two and into the hall. He screamed, cursing with the clicks and whistles of his native tongue.

Shirley and the unit secretary, who had remained behind at the nurse's station, screamed in unison, presumably at the alien head sticking out of the wall.

It took us a few minutes to extricate the Enochian and put him back on the stretcher. He had settled down by then.

"All right, let's try this again," I said. "You can tell me all about the plot to kill President Gamble later. But first, what is your name?"

He rubbed his head. "Dingo."

"Dingo?" I repeated.

"Yeah, Dingo. You gotta problem with Dingo?"

I shook my head. "No, no problem. Just want to get it right, Dingo."

"And don't start singing that song. I hate that song." He

started singing a familiar tune. " 'D-I-N-G-O, D-I-N-G-O, D-I-N-G-O, and Dingo was his name-O.' " Dingo shuddered in revulsion.

I shuddered at his singing. Enochians can't carry a tune.

"How long have you been in New Orleans?"

"About two months, but I've lived among humans for the last six years." He puffed his sagging jowls, the Enochian shrug. "I got tired of the damn reservation."

That explained his penchant for street talk and the lack of an accent. "Well, let's finish this exam and have Dr. Richards check you out."

I asked him all the old, familiar questions, which he answered in monosyllables. *Good, so far, according to plan,* I thought. I finished the initial examination and charted the results as I stood in Dingo's room.

"Dr. Richards has ordered a CT scan of your head, just to see if there's anything in there," I said. Dingo either ignored the joke or didn't understand. He just stared at me, a curious look on his face. I had some experience reading the reactions of Enochians during the War. Dingo looked worried. "What's eating you, Dingo? What's the problem?"

"You probably think I'm nuts, but I'm serious about the plot against the President," Dingo said, puffing his jowls. "And they are going to blame the Enochians, so they can restart the damn war."

I bit down on my pen. I didn't like what I was hearing. I liked the fact that I believed him even less. As to why I believed him, I couldn't say for sure, but, working in the emergency room, you caught the feel of lies and truth. I guess it just felt like truth.

"I've got to get out of here and warn my people," Dingo said. "They'll be slaughtered if the assassination takes place."

"Who's planning this?"

23

Dingo looked me over in much the same way my Little Old Lady had appraised me earlier in the night. I wondered if I measured up, or if he just had nowhere else to turn. "You look old enough to have been in the War," he said at last.

I said I had been an intelligence officer. I knew that I had impressed him. He smiled, which looked like a jagged cut across his face, revealing large ripping teeth, but I knew that the bicuspids were made for grinding like those of humans.

"Then, you know the Lanaka," Dingo said.

"The feared secret police of the Enochians? Hell yes, I know them. They killed as many of you guys as we did."

"The Lanaka are here on Earth." He motioned me closer. "I met with one the other day and he tried to get me to do the job. I said no, and he tried to kill me." Dingo stopped at the look on my face. "You don't believe." It was an accusation.

I hesitated. Something in what he said bothered me. It had the ring of truth, but it also had the ring of too many of the paranoid fantasies that waltzed through these doors every night. Maybe Dingo had been around humans too long.

Dingo closed his eyes, which meant he would not talk to me any longer. I had failed him. I was rejected.

Back at the nursing station, I picked up the chart to my LOL and saw that Richards had told her to take a gas pill for the pain and not to try an enema for another twenty-four hours. If the constipation was not better, she was to go see her doctor on Friday morning.

As I read her the discharge instructions and gave her the prescription, my mind went over what Dingo had said. The Lanaka were on Earth. If the Lanaka were on Earth, then the Enochians in New Mexico had more to worry about than any human did. But what if the Lanaka wanted the Enochian-Human conflict to continue for one reason or another? What if they could kill the President? What if Dingo was telling the truth and not just living out a paranoid fantasy? Were Enochians capable of the same types of mental illnesses that humans were?

Mrs. Winter stopped talking and I told her goodbye, knowing she would be back in the next month or two. I went to check on Dingo.

Room two proved empty, except for a discarded gown, so I guessed that he was in CT. But as I went back to the nurse's station, I glanced at the monitor and saw the CT tech getting out of his car.

"Larry, is the CT tech just getting here?"

"Yeah," he said without looking up from his magazine.

"Have you seen Dingo?" I asked. Larry looked at me, blankly. "The alien."

"Oh, him," Larry said. "I saw him leaving about five minutes ago. He said he had to kill the President or something." Larry went back to his magazine.

Something about my encounter with Dingo the Enochian bothered me, but I shrugged it off. It was five-thirty and I would be off work for seven glorious days in less than two hours. But I couldn't get Dingo off my mind. Or the Lanaka.

The rest of the night passed without major trauma. We stayed busy, not a kick-ass busy, but busy enough that Dingo slipped my mind. An hour after Dingo left, a young woman rolled in the door doubled over in lower abdominal pain. Tenderness in the right lower quadrant made me suspect appendicitis. Dr. Richards confirmed the diagnosis. A screaming baby came in sporting an ear infection. The

25

regular clinic patients arrived, milling around the waiting room as the day shift came in, one by one.

As I was clocking out, one of the RNs stopped me and told me that her child loved that song and sang it constantly. I hadn't realized I had been singing.

"D-I-N-G-O and Dingo was his name-O."

2

I dreamed Dingo had put my head in a metal container and was beating it with a concrete block. I awoke with a start but the banging did not cease. I mumbled an expletive or two and glared at the clock—ten-thirty. I had been asleep less than two hours and some fool was knocking on my door.

Throwing off the covers, I sat on the edge of the bed trying to get my bearings. Last night's scrubs were at my feet, so I put on the bottoms and stumbled to the door. Looking out of the peephole, I saw an attractive, if somewhat severe-looking, woman pounding the door. Her hair flowed away from her face, giving her long jaw an angular look. Blue eyes peered at the door with cold detachment. Someone stood behind her, but she blocked my view. She raised her hand and beat on the door again. The banging stopped when she heard me unlock the door.

Flinging the door open, I glared at the intruders. "This had better be damned important, or I'm going to throw your butt down those stairs," I said, putting an attitude with the words.

The woman did not appear to be impressed as she pushed her way past me. Another figure followed her, covered from head to toe in winter attire of the sort you don't normally see in New Orleans, even in January. I caught a whiff of a familiar odor.

"Do come in," I said, sarcasm dripping from the words.

"We're sorry to bother you, Mr. Stimson, but my name

27

is Captain Valerie Barnett of the United States Secret Service," she said.

Barnett spoke with no trace of emotion as she showed me her ID while glancing around the living room of my apartment which, after seven straight days of work, was a mess: glasses on the coffee table, assorted books and newspapers littering the floor beside my favorite chair. Captain Barnett paid no attention to the clutter. She was trying to recognize any potential threat to her or her companion.

"I'm sorry I was so abrupt, Captain," I said, trying to sound less threatening. One thing I did not need was problems with the Secret Service. "Why don't you and your Enochian friend sit down?"

Barnett stiffened, but otherwise betrayed no further reaction. She glanced behind her at the still-covered figure of the alien. The figure was short for an Enochian, but I was sure of the smell.

I answered her unspoken question. "I became quite familiar with the aliens during my stint in the War, particularly the smell," I said, smiling at the covered figure.

Barnett raised an eyebrow. "You don't like Enochians." It was a statement rather than a question.

I shrugged. "They killed my wife, during the War," I said with little emotion. "A civilian casualty, but I suppose in my intelligence unit I was responsible for many Enochian civilian casualties. I've made my own peace with them. I probably recognized this fellow's well-hidden smell because of Dingo, which I suppose is why you're here."

Barnett raised both eyebrows this time, which seemed to indicate that she was flabbergasted that I was able to discern the purpose for her visit. "That is precisely why we are here, Mr. Stimson," she said, turning to the alien. "This is Rafta, a representative of the Lanaka."

28

It was my turn to be flabbergasted. Our Secret Service working with the Lanaka? Barnett continued talking, but I wasn't listening.

The Enochian, Rafta, pulled back the hood on the jacket. He was slightly bluer than Dingo and not as proportionally built. I wondered if he was deformed in some way. I imagined that he had been quite bullied by other, larger Enochian children as a child. I made a mental note that this Enochian could be dangerous, in particular if he felt that he had to prove that he was as big as the rest. *Probably why he joined the Lanaka,* I thought. Not for the first time in my life, I chided myself for thinking of Enochians in human terms, regardless of how human they sometimes acted.

"Mr. Stimson," Barnett said with a frown, showing her displeasure at my distraction, "if I could have your attention, this interview will not last long."

"Captain Barnett, I'm sorry. I haven't had any sleep and I am interested in your friend here." I stared at the Enochian. The alien did not speak or move.

Barnett sighed. "I can understand that, sir, but Mr. Rafta is here only to observe. My department is handling the investigation of this matter."

I nodded. "Okay, Captain, what can I do for you?" I tore my eyes away from Rafta.

She opened her notebook. "Last night, at 0315, an alien was brought into the Memorial Hospital ER making accusations about killing the President." She stopped to take a breath.

"No ma'am, that is not exactly correct," I said, interrupting her. "Dingo said that the Lanaka was planning to kill President Gamble to restart the War."

Barnett's eyebrows furrowed as she flipped pages in her notebook. "That's not what one Lawrence Jones reported.

He said the Enochian left without treatment at 0343 and said, 'I'm going to kill the President.' "

"I don't know a Lawrence . . . oh, you mean Larry, the ER tech," I said, which brought a nod from Barnett. "Well, Larry was not with Dingo during the time period that I was. Besides, Dingo admitted drinking two fifths of whiskey before coming to the ER."

A soft, melodic voice came out of the alien's mouth, as it spoke for the first time. "You keep saying that the Enochian's name was Dingo. We have records for all of the Earth names taken by the Rejected, and Dingo is not among them."

I shrugged. "Dingo was his name-O. At least, that's what he said." A thought hit me. Sometimes, I am able to keep thoughts to myself, but I was tired. "If you have the taken names of all the rejected aliens that your government left behind, then you must have pretty good access to the reservation. It's been my impression that you guys just plain left, eight years ago."

The alien did not respond, but Captain Barnett did. "Mr. Stimson, back to the matter at hand. Are you saying that this Enochian, uh Dingo, did not threaten the life of the President of the United States?"

"Yep, that's what I'm saying. Dingo said the Lanaka was the real threat to both the President and the Rejected."

"An obvious drunken paranoid delusion," Rafta said.

I could tell that he had been among humans for a long time from his speech patterns. *How much is going on that we the public don't know about?* I mused.

"The thought did cross my mind," I said. "I see a lot of strange people at three o'clock in the morning. Keeps me on my toes." I smiled.

Barnett closed her book with a snap. "Thank you for

your time, Mr. Stimson." A hint of a smile crossed her face. I was right. She was attractive. "We're sorry to have disturbed you."

"No problem, Captain," I said as I walked them to the door. I stopped and focused on the alien. "Rafta, how long have you been on Earth this time?"

"I've been here only two weeks," the smooth, alien voice said.

I nodded. "Earth, New Orleans in particular, has many activities and places to visit that can be enjoyable," I said. "You don't even have to invade the place to enjoy them."

Barnett shot me a reproving look.

"If you have any other questions, Captain, can they hold until after four p.m.?" I smiled as I asked the question.

"I think that will be all, Mr. Stimson. Sorry to have bothered you." They left and I slammed the door closed.

I wondered why Rafta, the small Enochian, had lied about just getting to Earth. Rafta was just as comfortable with human contact as Dingo had been. Either Rafta had been on Earth for a long while, or the Enochians had kept some of the missing personnel we never recovered. There had been rumors.

At that moment, I was too tired to think about it. I looked at the clock, fell into bed, and went right back to sleep. This time I dreamed that the little Enochian, Rafta of the Lanaka, was trying to kill me. It seemed like a premonition.

3

Someone was banging on my door again. I felt like I had only just put my head back down on the pillow, but the clock said it was almost one in the afternoon. I mumbled a few curses about people who did not work night shift under my breath while sliding into my scrub bottoms. Stumbling to the door, I ripped it open.

"What?" I admit that I screamed at the intruder. Not getting my sleep makes me a bit edgy.

The face staring at me was familiar, but my groggy mind could not place it. The man grinned a fake grin at me and said, "Well, Captain Stimson, I see growing a few years older hasn't helped your attitude much."

I blinked twice and made my eyes focus on the grinning face and then at the other man who had joined him at the door. I realized that I recognized them both. The man grinning at me was Rafe Boudreau, my commanding officer during the War. Boudreau had turned his high-profile military career into a six-year term as the junior senator from Louisiana.

Coiffed silver hair lay perfect on Boudreau's head. Though short, he carried himself with confidence and bravado, a perfect example of the New Army general that he was in the War. As a politician, the same qualities, good looks and confidence, carried him through the election six years ago. Some political analysts even mentioned his name as a challenger to President Gamble's next election.

The man behind him was Denny Lolich, a former officer

32

under my command, at least until I tried to have him court-martialed for cruelty to the Enochians. General Boudreau interceded on Lolich's behalf and transferred him to his personal staff as a bodyguard. He wasn't the meaty type of bodyguard, meant to intimidate people. Lolich was my size, more or less, with broader shoulders and an irritating smirk. From experience, I knew he had no conscience and few, if any, ethics. He didn't seem to fit inside Boudreau's great and heroic public persona. Lolich was a lowlife, and dangerous. I wondered what uses Boudreau found for him in the world of politics.

"Don't old Army buddies get to come inside?" Boudreau widened his grin.

We weren't buddies and he knew it. Boudreau had sanctioned the release of a virus to kill the Enochians, and then left me hanging out to dry when his superiors and Congress wanted a scapegoat for what was considered a war crime. I was acquitted, but not with Boudreau's help.

I shook my head to fight off fatigue. "Come on in," I said, turning away from the door. "Everybody else is." I motioned toward the couch. "Have a seat. You want coffee?"

They moved toward the couch, but continued to stand. "I do not have time for coffee, Captain," Boudreau said. "I'm here because I need your help locating an alien who was last seen in the emergency room where you work. Did you work last night?"

I rubbed my hand through my thinning hair. "Yeah, I worked," I said, still feeling groggy after two short periods of sleep. "This damn Enochian is not only very popular, he's interrupting my sleep. The Secret Service just left."

I didn't mention Rafta of the Lanaka. I think I trusted the Lanaka more than I trusted Boudreau. At least with the Lanaka, you knew where things stood. Boudreau didn't react to the news of the Secret Service.

I glanced at Lolich, who was standing beside Boudreau, remembering his brutal treatment of the Enochians at the Unit. "You want this alien as a plaything for Lolich?" I asked, watching Lolich stiffen at my reference to his past actions. No, he had never forgiven me for trying to send him to the stockade.

I'd caught Lolich in an Enochian cell with two of his guards. Pieces of blue flesh lay on the floor, and I saw a grinning Lolich using his knife to carve more. I stopped their "interrogation," but not soon enough. The Enochian died from the torture. The fact that I killed many more of the aliens did not stop me from bringing charges. Lolich had enjoyed his job a bit too much.

"Captain—" Boudreau began, but I interrupted him.

"I'm not a captain anymore and you're damn well not my general," I said, measuring my words and expelling them with force. "Hell, as far as I'm concerned, you're not even my senator. I sure didn't vote for you."

Boudreau's smile never faded, but I saw a hint of anger in his eyes. Lolich stiffened and took a step toward me. I turned to the side to give the bodyguard less of a target if he tried anything. I might be older, but I've stayed up to date on some of my training, which comes in quite handy working in the emergency room. Boudreau made a subtle hand gesture toward Lolich, who relaxed. I stayed tense, wanting them out of my apartment.

Boudreau resumed talking. "I want your help, Cap . . . uh, Stimson. This alien is spreading rumors, and we want to talk to him."

I glared at Lolich, knowing that Dingo would be at the end of a fire poker if Boudreau let Lolich do the talking. I shook my head. "Boudreau, I don't know where the alien went. And I frankly don't give a damn, especially about helping you." I walked to the door and opened it. "Now, if you don't mind, and even if you do, the two of you are leaving and I'm going back to sleep."

"You haven't changed, have you, Roger?" Boudreau shook his head, but walked toward the door. He stopped in front of me. "You always did do things the hard way."

"If your way is the easy way, then the hard way is my only choice," I said.

Boudreau frowned. "I thought maybe we could put the past behind us. I could be in a position to help you one day." The plastic smile returned.

"Not likely, Boudreau," I said. "The last time I had anything to do with you, I almost went to the stockade, and you were the chief witness against me. Get out!"

Boudreau lost his smile. He glared for a few seconds, and then walked out of the door.

Lolich followed, but stopped in front of me. "We'll see each other again, Stimson," he said in a controlled and menacing voice. "I promise you that."

"Oh, I can't wait to see your lovely face again, Lolich." I smiled as I spoke. "It reminds me so much of the end result of an enema." He snorted and left.

I thought about what Boudreau said, that I always did things the hard way, and wondered what he meant. Was the hard way opposing anything that Boudreau wanted? What type of damage could a United States Senator do to a lowly emergency room nurse? I shrugged and sighed.

I didn't worry about it too much. Boudreau had always been a blowhard who only looked out for his own ass, which of course made him into the perfect politician. I went back into the bedroom and got back into bed, swearing I would kill the next person who woke me.

4

The sun sank beneath a bank of clouds as I looked out of my window. The radio blasted in my ear after three hours of fitful, but uninterrupted sleep. Images of human and Enochian bodies flashed through my mind. Dingo and Rafta laughed at the devastation. I rubbed my face, banishing the nightmares and dreams. I turned down the radio's volume and tuned to the local news channel.

"Police are uncertain as to the motive of the killing, or why an Enochian was even in the New Orleans area, but a full investigation has been promised into the death of the alien, according to New Orleans Police Department Homicide Detective Brian Devereaux," the newscaster said. "In other news, plans for the Presidential trip to New Orleans next Monday afternoon . . ." I blinked hard, trying to make sense of what I had just heard, tuning out the rest of the news.

Damn, I said to myself. *After eight years of the peace and calm of the ER, now I've got aliens pouring out of my ass again.* It sure sounded like Dingo, or maybe Rafta, had been killed. *Probably by one of those people from that xenophobic hate group, the Sons of Earth.*

I hadn't thought of the Sons of Earth in years. They sprang up at the end of the War, paranoid and wary of the New Mexico Enochian Reservation of the Rejected. The Sons of Earth's leader, James Williams, gained much of his notoriety by leading public outrage at my court-martial, a fact that never set real well with me. I'd never met Williams,

36

but knew it would not be a joyful experience for him if I ever did. I switched off the radio.

I got up from the bed and stumbled to the kitchen to start my coffee. My answering machine blinked, so I punched the button as I waited for the coffee to brew. The first of the two messages was a hang-up, but the second one woke me without the coffee.

"This is Brian Devereaux, from the NOPD. I need to see Roger Stimson about a dead Enochian. We have reason to believe you may have been the last person to talk to him." The detective left his number for me to return the call. I poured my coffee and sat at the kitchen table, somewhat stunned by the events of the last fifteen hours. Then I dialed the number.

"NOPD Homicide," said a bored voice.

"Brian Devereaux, please," I said. "I'm returning his call."

"May I say who's calling?"

"Roger Stimson."

It didn't take Devereaux long to get on the line. With a slight Cajun accent that reminds other southerners of the Bronx, Devereaux answered the phone. "Mr. Stimson, thank you for returning my call. I'd like to ask you a few questions if I may?"

I voiced my consent, and he asked me pretty much what Barnett and the small Enochian had asked me earlier in the day. I recounted the story to him, but left out any mention of Rafta. If the Secret Service wanted people to know they were working with the Lanaka, they'd tell them.

"The paramedics said that the alien had been in a fight, hit in the head with a concrete block, and he was still alive?" he asked.

It was obvious that Devereaux had seen what a concrete block can do to a human skull; so had I. "Detective,

Enochians have a much thicker skeletal system than we do," I answered him. "It would probably take a jackhammer ten minutes to get to their brain."

"Uh-huh. Okay, thank you, Mr. Stimson." I started to say goodbye, when he said, "Oh, by the way, I hate to ask you this, but we don't seem to have anyone who can identify the body . . ." He let the words trail off.

I knew what he was asking. "Tell me how to get to the morgue," I said, sighing. "I'm not sure that I can help you, but I have seen a few more of these things than most folks."

"You were in the War?"

"I served in the Sahara theatre," I said. "Got up close with quite a few Enochians."

I could hear him sigh. "Me, too," Devereaux said. "We probably swallowed some of the same sand." There was an odd silence over the phone as two veterans recalled memories of horror. "Thanks for doing this, Mr. Stimson."

"No problem, Detective. I just woke, so give me about an hour or so." We hung up.

Even in January, without Mardi Gras or the Super Bowl, New Orleans traffic confounded most drivers. I've always been a southerner and I am convinced that the majority of my fellow southern drivers still do not know how to drive on the interstate and that their tractors do not have signals installed in them.

Devereaux met me at the door of the police station and took me downstairs to where the Enochian body was stored. He was an overweight cop who had been off the beat too long and probably partook of too much of the Cajun food, but his penetrating eyes belied the friendly manner in which he spoke. I felt as though he wondered how many lies I had told him. Occupational hazard I guess, because I do the same thing in the ER.

"Thanks, again, Mr. Stimson. This way we can positively identify that this was the same alien who was in the ER last night." Devereaux opened the door to the room and I saw several bodies lying on tables in the morgue.

I nodded at the coroner who happened to be there. He nodded back, not knowing who I was, but knowing that he probably did not like me. He was right; he didn't like me. I was one of the people who called him at home at three in the morning when we had a dead body in the ER. Devereaux and I followed the coroner to a wall in the far back.

Formaldehyde saturated everything, but its smell mixed with bleach to provide an even more noxious odor. We walked past a young woman who stared without seeing the ceiling. Another table stood empty as we made our way to the rows of silver doors. The coroner tapped on one of the doors. I hoped nothing would tap back. He grabbed the handle and pulled, revealing a small cubicle that contained a body. With effort, he hauled out the slab.

Devereaux pulled back the sheet and I looked at an alien face for the third time in the last day. It looked like Dingo, but I wasn't sure. "You know, it's been eight years since . . . since I've seen one of these things dead or alive. Why so many in so short a space of time?" I regretted my words almost before I stopped speaking.

Devereaux was startled. "You mean this isn't the same alien?"

"Pull the sheet back a little more," I told him, ignoring his question. "These things look as different dead as humans do."

"Yeah, I know," Devereaux said. "I've had family members refuse to identify a victim, because it didn't look like their loved one. Sort of sad, really."

Devereaux pulled the sheet down to the waist. There was no tattoo on this alien's body. It was not Dingo. *What the hell is going on here?* I asked myself. My thoughts went back to Dingo and what he told me last night. Someone's going to assassinate the President and blame it on the Rejected to restart the War. I wanted some answers. I looked at the body again. This was definitely the third Enochian I had seen today. This dead thing was not Dingo.

"That's him," I said, lying to Devereaux. "That's the Enochian who called himself Dingo."

Devereaux looked relieved. "Damn, I thought for a second we had two aliens running around out there," he said. "You're sure this is him?"

I nodded. I didn't tell Devereaux that he had two live aliens in his city, not including this dead one. I didn't want to worry the man.

Devereaux led me out of the morgue and to the street, thanking me for my help. He gave me his card, which I put in my pocket.

"Look, if you think of anything else, give me a call," Devereaux said as he looked in my eyes. I think he knew I had not told him everything. His eyes penetrated into my brain. Had I not turned away from him, I just might have confessed to lying and maybe a murder or two just to get those eyes off me.

I flopped into my car and sat there for a moment. I wanted answers, but not at the cost of interfering with a murder investigation. Besides, if I tried to find anything out, I'd probably have the Ice Queen of the Secret Service breathing down my neck, as well as that good old dumb Cajun boy, Devereaux. I started the car and pulled out of the parking space. Looking in my rearview mirror, I saw Devereaux's piercing eyes as he watched me drive away.

5

Since the end of the War, I'd avoided having anything to do with Enochians. The pain was too much; the memories were too sad. I guess I'm not unlike most of the veterans who saw friends slaughtered at the hands of the unrelenting alien attack, but the last twenty-four hours had brought to my mind the question that we in the intelligence unit had asked over and over again.

Why hadn't the Enochians just destroyed us with their superior technology when they first arrived, rather than letting us group together as a planet and run them out of the solar system? I pondered that question at the library near my apartment, looking for books on the culture of the aliens. I didn't know if the answer was likely to be found in books. Probably not, I decided, but I had aliens popping out at me everywhere. I checked out a couple of books on the Enochians and went home.

Most of the information in the books was pretty dry and, with my sleep having been interrupted this morning, I was having a hard time staying awake. I picked up a book written by Denise Windham—a disgraced sociologist living in Midland, Texas, according to the book cover—which dealt directly with the Rejected Enochians. She'd lived on the reservation with the approval of the Rejected Enochian Prefect and with the approval of the United States government. It was a well-written sociological study of the aliens from the inside. No one before or since had been given the access that Windham received. Since writing her book, Windham had become the patron saint of the Sons of Earth movement, much to her consternation, according to interviews I had seen.

However, in her writing, she displayed a real fascination and empathy for the Rejected on the New Mexico reservation. She also took a shot at answering my question as to why they hadn't seemed to use all of the tools at their disposal for the purpose of winning the Enochian-Human War. The Enochians never intended to defeat us, she wrote.

"The alien society lives by the adage of, 'You can never know your friends, unless they were once your enemies.' " I read that statement three times, a knot forming in my stomach, one I had hoped never to feel again, but on it came. The Enochians never intended to win the war with us. They were just testing our capabilities.

I closed the book, putting it on the table beside my bed, and rubbed my eyes. Guilt flooded into me with more strength than it had in years. "How the hell were we supposed to know?" I said to the book. "We were fighting for our lives." I didn't expect to sleep with my mind dwelling on past misfortunes, yet I could feel myself slipping away.

But my subconscious didn't let me off that easy.

I was in uniform as the intelligence officer for the Bio-Chem Warfare Unit. I landed the job because of my background in biochemistry. After earning a degree in Biochemistry at South Alabama, I spent four years paying back the ROTC with a hitch in the Army, where I went through rigorous training in biological and chemical warfare. After graduation, I finished a Master's at Tulane, but while I was preparing for my doctoral studies, the Enochians landed in the Sahara and I received a call-up from inactive reserve.

The attacks started with the landing. Cities would

be surgically strafed, avoiding major damage, but inflicting civilian casualties. When we responded, the Enochians attacked the troops with more determination. The aliens rebuffed all efforts at negotiation with a terse, "As of now, we have nothing to discuss." Egyptian, Libyan, and Moroccan troops attacked the Saharan Base and managed some successes, but the Enochians regained their positions and began pushing toward Tripoli, Cairo, and Marrakech. An alien ship unloaded a barrage on Los Angeles, killing hundreds of thousands. Similar attacks occurred in Europe, Asia, South America, and Africa, but not to the extent of the Los Angeles Massacre. The Los Angeles attack killed a lot of people and brought with it the outrage of the United States populace, and the attacks on civilian centers throughout the world brought cohesiveness to human governments, motivating and uniting a world previously at odds with itself. The United Nations mobilized and fought.

The aliens controlled twenty percent of the landmass on Earth. My unit moved to the front in order to have a steady supply of the alien prisoners. We had to find out how they ticked. I relived the discovery of the mutated gene in their system that, if we pushed it the right way, would be close to one hundred percent fatal to them. My team developed a virus that activated the mutation. Since our biologies were so different, the alien virus would not harm humans.

On the orders of General Boudreau, I released the virus, which began debilitating and killing the Enochian invaders. The virus attacked the Enochian nervous system, eating away at internal tissue. Their organs became liquefied in much the same way the

Ebola virus attacks human physiology. Whole armies died in the field. Seeing the devastation, my team isolated the virus again and developed an antidote, much to the chagrin of my commanding officer, General Boudreau.

Two weeks later, the Enochians pulled out and we released a number of their prisoners. I pleaded with Boudreau to allow the transfer of the antidote. When he denied my request, I took matters into my own hands. My guilt had deepened from the day we'd released the virus. Smuggling the antidote to the Enochians through one of their prisoners did not assuage my responsibility.

The historical nature of the dream changed. I stood alone in a white room of unknowable dimensions. I stared upward as a disembodied voice spoke down to me.

"How many of my people did you kill?" it asked. I recognized Dingo's voice.

"We were at war, damn it. And we were losing."

"How many died?" The voice insisted on an answer.

Breathing became difficult for me. I wanted to protest, to say that we didn't know that this was some sort of test. We were fighting a war of survival, or so we thought, but I bowed my head, fighting the guilt that rushed through me. "Millions, at least," I whispered. "Possibly billions, if the virus made it back to your homeworld. I don't really know."

6

I sat up in bed, covered in sweat on the cold night, wondering what had awakened me. The phone rang again. I answered it.

"Roger, you've got to get out of town."

I recognized the voice. It was Shirley from the ER. Rather than her normal cynical tone, Shirley's voice held a shrill quality I was not used to hearing. Something frightened her. "Shirl, why are you calling me at this time of the morning?" I looked at the clock. Yep, it was morning, early morning. "It's three o'clock, woman. Why aren't you asleep? What's wrong?"

"Shut up and listen to me," she said, almost hysterical. "Dr. Richards is dead. Murdered. So is Larry. My husband just shot at something that looked a lot like that thing that came into the ER last night."

"Whoa, what do you mean that Larry and the Doc are dead?" I was having trouble comprehending her. "What thing that came . . ." I stopped. Dingo.

"The alien, you idiot," she screamed, her voice even more shrill. "It murdered Larry and Richards. Get the hell out—" Shirley's phone went dead.

I sat in bed, stunned. I tried calling Shirley back, but a computer-generated voice said there was trouble on that line. *You don't know the half of it,* I thought.

I got out of bed and put on some clothes. Turning on the hall light, I looked for the .45 in my closet. Shirley's phone call spooked me. I had never known her to pull practical jokes. The fear in her voice sounded genuine. Too many strange things had happened since Dingo came to the Emergency Room.

I found the gun and inspected it. It was clean, oiled, and had not been fired in over eight years. I don't know why I had even kept it, but for now, I felt better with it in my hand. I took a deep breath. *Now where did I put those magazines?* I glanced around the bedroom, trying to remember the hiding place. I never kept a loaded gun, figuring someone would find it and use it on me before I had the chance to respond. I walked out of the bedroom and remembered. *Oh yeah,* I thought, *kitchen cabinet.*

As I loaded the pistol, the phone rang again. I picked up the kitchen extension. "Shirley?"

It wasn't Shirley.

"Mr. Stimson? This is Brian Devereaux of the NOPD. Sorry to call so late, but I'm afraid I have some rather disturbing news for you, sir." He hesitated. I could hear people talking and highway noise in the background.

Shirley was right, I thought. *They're all dead.*

"Mr. Stimson, arc you there?" Devereaux sounded tired and pissed.

"Yeah, Detective, I'm here." My mind tried to reject what was happening.

"I've been investigating multiple homicides all night. I didn't put the victims together until this last call." Devereaux hesitated again. I knew what came next, but I waited for Devereaux to tell me. "Do you know a Dr. Stephen Richards and a Lawrence Jones?"

"They're dead, aren't they, Detective?" I felt my stomach trying to knot up on me again. Was I somehow responsible for their deaths, however indirectly?

"Uh, how did you know?"

"Someone is killing everyone who was in the ER last night when that damn alien came in," I said, harshness bringing an edge to my voice. I knew that Shirley's phone had not gone dead naturally. *Two more souls on my conscience,* I thought. "I think there are two more victims in Algiers."

"What happened?" Devereaux's voice sounded strained, as if he had trouble dealing with all the death in his city.

"Shirley Nichols just called and said something was outside their house," I said. "She told me about Larry and Dr. Richards."

"Damn it," he said. "Do you know the address?" I gave it to him. "Hold on." The phone dropped from his hand and I heard a muffled voice for a moment.

"I've got a car on the way," he said. "So that leaves the other RN and clerk, right?" Devereaux spoke without emotion, but something told me that these murders really pissed him off.

Wait until I tell him that I lied to him earlier tonight, I thought. *He's really going to like that.*

"Don't forget the two EMTs," I said, remembering that they had originally reported Dingo's story of the alleged assassination plot. "Dingo told them the same story he told us."

"That's what put two and two together for me," Devereaux said. "The EMTs were found in their ambulance about forty-five minutes ago. They had both been shot once in the back of the head. Look, I'm sending a car over to your apartment. I want you to go with them."

A noise outside, the thud of feet hitting wooden planks on my balcony, took my attention away from the phone call. "Hold on for a minute, Detective."

"Stimson," Devereaux said. "Wait!"

I laid the phone on the table and went into the dining

area to get a better look. I was right. A silhouetted figure stood on the balcony, holding something. A four-fingered hand reached toward the door and found it locked. I heard the shattering of glass and the characteristic sound of automatic weapons fire. I dropped to the floor for cover and fired my pistol twice at the figure. One round hit the wall, but I thought the other might have found the intruder.

I heard a yelp, more of anger than pain, and the outlined figure jumped flat-footed from my second-story balcony. I was sweating and shaking, but unharmed from the attack. *That was not a human,* I thought. *I am certain that was an Enochian.*

I stood to go back toward the kitchen to tell Devereaux what had happened, when I heard the thud of someone landing on my balcony for a second time. I heard more breaking glass and saw a small, round object flying into my living room. The Enochian intruder jumped from the balcony. I dove into the kitchen before the grenade blew up, throwing shrapnel everywhere.

I hurt all over from the concussion of the explosion and, just before losing consciousness, I remembered that the Enochian figure was short and squat.

7

Someone shook my shoulder, asking if I was all right. *Hell no, I'm not all right,* I screamed at the idiot in my mind. *Some fool just tried to kill me.* When the person ran his knuckles hard up and down my breastbone, I found my voice.

"Stop that shit, will you?" I said. "That hurt."

Pam Susskind, a shorthaired, blond paramedic, smiled. My pain reflected in her green eyes. When Pam smiled, those eyes twinkled. Right now, they showed concern.

"It was supposed to hurt, Roger," she said. "You needed to wake up." I tried to sit up, but Pam pushed me back down. "You're not going anywhere or even moving, buddy boy, until a doctor says you can."

I lay back down and didn't argue. My head pounded all the way to my toenails. Being blown up by a grenade rather did that to a person. "Where am I?" Her partner had grabbed my head, immobilizing my cervical spine, so I couldn't look around. "Take it easy, guy," I said to him. "I'm going to cooperate."

"You're in what is left of your apartment," said a male voice from behind me. "I don't think renter's insurance is going to cover an explosion from a grenade." Detective Devereaux walked into my line of vision. "And I wish you had cooperated more with me earlier tonight." Devereaux paused as he glared. He knew I had lied to him.

He spoke to Pam, who was taking my pulse and respirations. "Can I talk to him while you work on him?"

She shrugged. "Sure, but he needs to remain still." She put her face over mine to make sure I saw the seriousness in her eyes. "If you move, I'll slap you on that backboard and leave you there for so long, you'll think your back has turned to fiberglass. Understand?" I nodded.

"Good," she said. "I'll never forgive you if you screw up your C-spine and die on me. Besides, you can't die yet. You still owe me a dinner." Pam was a nice kid. At twenty-eight, she was ten years my junior. We had gone out a few times, but only as friends.

"After this, I owe you two dinners."

"Sorry to interrupt the banter between you two love-birds, but I've got a murder spree to investigate," Devereaux said, not looking real pleased. "Now, Mr. Stimson, you are going to tell me the whole truth. You know, the major part of what you left out earlier tonight. Or, when you get out of the hospital, you're not going to have to worry about a place to live."

I took a deep breath and told him everything he already knew about the Enochian Dingo's visit to the ER yesterday morning.

"I know all that shit, and I've already figured out that the murders of your coworkers and the attempt on your life are related to that," Devereaux said. He leaned over and put his nose about one inch from mine. I could feel his fat hand pressing on my chest as he screamed into my face. "What the hell have you left out of your story?"

"Hey, get off my patient," Pam yelled. I felt the pressure lift off my chest and I gasped for air.

Devereaux turned to confront Pam. "Look, lady, I've got a dead alien, a dead doctor, a dead nurse, and two dead EMTs, and this asshole is withholding information. If he wasn't already hurt, I'd beat the information out of him."

Devereaux gasped for air after his tirade. I thought he might hit her.

Pam did not back off. "No, you look, fat boy, if you screw up his damn spine, he could die before he has a chance to answer you." Pam gave up about eighty pounds and ten inches to Devereaux, but my money would have been on her at that moment.

Don't underestimate the cop, a little voice told me.

"Pam, it's all right," I said. "I can handle it. Detective, you probably do not want to get that upset. At your weight, your blood pressure is probably already high. If you stroke out, then you'll never know what a real criminal I am."

I could hear Devereaux still breathing hard, but he turned from Pam and looked at me. Before he could ask any more questions, I continued, "Detective, you said a nurse was dead. Was it Shirley?"

"Yeah, I sent a patrol car over there, while I came over here," Devereaux said. His voice was calm, as if he had not just exploded. "Her husband is also dead. You're the only one they tried to blow up."

I sighed and tried to nod, but couldn't move my head. "After work, Thursday morning, a Secret Service agent and an Enochian came to my door, asking questions about the story Dingo told concerning an assassination attempt."

Devereaux muttered under his breath. "Damn it, why can't people just tell me everything when I first ask them to? My job would get a whole lot easier." He sighed and studied me. "Another alien?" I tried to nod again but the emergency medical technician stopped me by holding my neck. "Okay, so we've got two aliens involved with this," Devereaux said. "The dead one you call Dingo and the one with the Secret Service." He ticked off the number of aliens in New Orleans with his left hand.

"No, we have at least three aliens," I said, sighing. "The one in your morgue is not Dingo. He doesn't have the tattoo."

"Tattoo?" Devereaux asked. "What damn tattoo?"

"It showed an exploding Earth and a smiley face," I said. "I have no clue who that alien in the morgue is, but I know it's not Dingo."

Devereaux shook his head and was quiet for the moment. He looked at the two fingers representing two aliens and added a third. He stared at me, and I could tell he was thinking. I figured he was deciding how many ways he could charge me for obstruction of justice and withholding evidence. Or maybe he just wanted to get me in the back room with the rubber hose. If he tried that, I might surprise him. I kept up some of my skills from the Army.

"Why did you lie to me?"

"I don't know," I said. "I thought I might try to find Dingo and figure out just what the hell was going on." I didn't tell him that my guilt for past actions against the Enochians had anything to do with it.

Pam interrupted. "I'd like to get my patient ready for transport, if you don't mind," she said to Devereaux. "Like now, Detective."

"Just one more question for now," he said to me, ignoring Pam. "What was the Secret Service agent's name?"

"Barnett," I said. "Valerie Barnett, I think."

Devereaux nodded and wrote down the name. He got up and glared down at me. "Mr. Stimson, you and I have an appointment when the docs get through with you." He started to turn away.

"Oh, and the Enochian with her was not an average alien."

"Yeah?" Devereaux stopped and kneeled back down beside me.

"Yeah. He was much smaller in stature, like a dwarf or something, only five-ten. Barnett said his name was Rafta." I hesitated.

"What else?" he said, almost barking the question.

"Are you familiar with the Lanaka?" The look on his face told me that he was. "She said he was a Lanaka representative. He was also the shape I saw on my balcony right before my living room blew up."

"I want to get this man to the hospital." Pam stood, holding the backboard. Devereaux was looking past me and into his own past, I think. "Detective?"

"Yeah, go ahead." To me, he said, "Don't go anywhere. I'll talk to you later." Devereaux left my line of sight.

Pam and her partner bundled me up for the trip to the hospital. Pam did not bother me. I think she was mad because I had told her to butt out, even if I said it nicely. Okay, so I owe her three dinners.

I knew that I would be in the hospital only long enough for a few x-rays. The doctor said I was all right, and that I should stay out of any rooms with grenades exploding in them for at least the next forty-eight hours.

"I'll try," I said. "I'm not sure I can promise anything, though." He laughed and released me. My visit to my own ER would be joke fodder for years, after we got over the tragedy of the situation, but for now, there were at least six people dead because of a drunken alien. And someone had tried to make me number seven.

Enough is enough, I told myself. I knew what I was going to do. I was going to get answers, if I had to use a concrete block on that thick alien skull. I was going to find Dingo.

8

I was released from the ER around six-thirty and hitched a ride with a nurse at shift change. Thanking him, I trudged up the steps to my apartment. I tore down the police tape across my door and walked in. The living room presented the most damage, but there was no sign of a fire and everything below the bar that separated the dining/living room was all right. I didn't have an unbroken glass in the cabinets.

There were holes in all of the walls from the shrapnel, as it spread in all directions. I was lucky that I wasn't torn to shreds with the blast. The kitchen counters and shelving showed a lot of damage, so I guess they saved my life. I saw bits of shattered plates and shredded plastic glasses. I'd need new dinnerware. There were a lot of things for which I could be thankful, but I wasn't feeling particularly thankful.

I walked into the bedroom.

Devereaux sat on the edge of my bed reading the Denise Windham book on the Rejected Enochian culture. He did not look up as he spoke. "Poor woman had the misfortune of being right about the wrong thing," he said as he closed the book and threw it onto my bed. "She's right when she says the whole business of the Rejected could be nonsense. I think the whole damn bunch are spies for their homeworld masters."

I sighed and rubbed my temples. "What the hell do you want?" I didn't wait for an answer. "I'm tired, I'm angry, I'm frustrated, and I've got one shitfire of a headache. So what do you want?" I glared.

Devereaux ignored my outburst. "The grenade they threw up here wasn't incendiary, as you might could tell, since the complex didn't burn to the ground." He stood up and faced me. "In fact, it was of a type that was mothballed by the United Nations about twenty-five years back. They used to be called cluster bombs, and cut to pieces anyone and anything standing around them. Only people who have them now are collectors and paramilitary organizations." He searched my face for reaction. Finding none, he continued. "What do you know about the Sons of Earth?"

"Practically nothing," I said. "Why?"

"Because the leader of that group, James Williams, happens to be in New Orleans, and he is the largest known 'collector' of that particular type of ordinance," Devereaux said. "Whatcha wanna bet that we will find evidence that this particular device could have been from his private stock?"

I shook my head. "It doesn't make sense. That was an Enochian on my balcony last night. I saw him jump off and then back onto the railing. I can't see a xenophobic hate group employing an alien to do their dirty work."

"Hmm, maybe," Devereaux said. "That was the same alien who was with the Secret Service agent you met yesterday, who the Secret Service said doesn't exist."

"She wasn't Secret Service?" I said. "But she had credentials, and I've seen Secret Service credentials before."

"In the War?" he asked.

I nodded. "And in the last two weeks," I said. "Memorial is the best trauma emergency room in the city. Starting Sunday night, one of our trauma bays has been set aside in case the President needs attention." The thought that President Gamble might really need our services at Memorial unnerved me, if Dingo was right. I looked around my demolished apartment and shuddered. "The Secret Service made a few trips to set up security for the visit, so I've seen quite a few credentials in recent days."

"Well, I can get you IDs and credentials for anything, even the Lanaka," Devereaux said. He studied me again, waiting for a reaction. I said nothing.

Devereaux shrugged. "Well, just thought I'd let you know." He walked past me out of the bedroom and into the living room. Devereaux stopped and surveyed the destruction. "I don't think I'd stay here for a while." He chuckled. "Your landlord looked like he might want to kill you, too." He walked out of the door, but called back to me over his shoulder. "By the way, I didn't find your gun or ammunition in the top of your bedroom closet."

"Thanks."

"Don't mention it, really." Devereaux left.

I shut the door as best I could. Either I was no longer a suspect of any wrongdoing, according to Devereaux, or more likely, he was going to follow my every move. He knew I was going to go find Dingo.

Walking past the kitchen, I noticed that the answering machine was blinking at me. I punched the button.

"It's amazing this thing still works after the explosion," said a feminine voice on the recording. "This is Valerie Barnett, Mr. Stimson, and you will want to meet with me. By now, you should be wondering what this is all about. Considering your military record, I'd say you just might be interested in our project." The voice paused. In the background, I could hear her tell someone that she would be right there. "Meet me tonight at six in front of the Café Du Monde." She hung up.

Could be a trap, I thought, congratulating myself on a masterpiece of detective work. After all, her partner had already tried to kill me once. I knew too much, just from listening to a drunken alien.

I punched the reset on the tape and took a couple of steps toward the bedroom. A dark figure was standing in my way. I stopped, startled. "Who the hell are you?" I demanded.

A well-dressed fortyish woman stepped into the light and presented an ID badge that was emblazoned with the words "Secret Service" in nice bold letters. She had short hair and wore a conservative gray suit.

I shrugged, unimpressed. "I saw one of those things yesterday morning, as a matter of fact." I raised an eyebrow at her. "I hope your identification is a bit more authentic."

"Yes, Mr. Stimson," the woman said. "Devereaux told me. My name is Michelle Allen. The woman who visited you yesterday is an impostor."

I looked around my blown-up apartment. "Yeah, I guessed."

Allen glanced around and smiled. "I am investigating both the impostor and the threat to President Gamble's life," she said. "Would you mind telling me about your visit from the Enochian?"

"Which Enochian?" I wasn't sure if I could believe anyone at the moment and I wasn't feeling cooperative.

Allen remained calm. "Tell me about the alien in the emergency room."

"Not much to tell, really," I said. "He was brought in after an altercation and made a statement that the Lanaka was trying to restart the War by assassinating President Gamble. Dingo had been very drunk when he arrived."

She wrote notes on a small notepad. "Did you say Dingo?" She looked up and I nodded. "What can you tell me about Barnett and the other alien?"

"Barnett said she was investigating Dingo's supposed

threats on Gamble," I said. "An Enochian introduced to me by the name of Rafta accompanied her." I described him briefly.

"Uh-huh," she said. After she finished writing, she flipped the notepad shut.

"Does the Secret Service have a connection with the Enochians, or was that another lie from Barnett?"

Allen ignored my question. She kept her silence and looked around the room for a few seconds, then abruptly changed the subject. "Do you have any enemies, Mr. Stimson?"

I glanced around my apartment. "Well, I guess I do," I said. "This doesn't look like the work of a friend, now does it?"

Allen grimaced. "What about aliens who know about your *intelligence* background?"

A chill went through me. It figured that a Secret Service agent would have access to my military records. I didn't answer. I knew where Allen's line of thought was going.

"Didn't you tell Devereaux that an alien did this?" She swiped her arm toward the destruction in my living room.

"You don't think that the President is in any danger," I said. She didn't answer. "Well, what about the other killings last night?"

It was her turn to shrug. "New Orleans is a dangerous place, Mr. Stimson," Allen said. I knew that she'd made up her mind. "Thank you for your time, sir." She turned and left without another word. I shook my head as I watched her get into her car and leave the parking lot.

She doesn't believe me, I thought. *Why am I not surprised?*

I went to the bedroom and inspected my clothes, most of which were torn to threads by the shrapnel, but I found some things and packed them into a bag. On the shelf above my clothes, I found my .45, along with three boxes of ammunition. I figured that was why Devereaux was in my bedroom. A .32-caliber pistol and additional ammo lay beside it. Someone thought I might need a back-up.

Devereaux knew more about what was going on than I did. "Damn it, everybody knows more than I do," I said to Devereaux's pistol.

I was a puppet at the end of someone's string. I was tired of being a marionette for some unknown entity, but I had the feeling that everything was going to the puppet master's plan, including the thwarted attempt on my life. To find out what was going on here, I would have to follow the lead of the puppet master. Eventually, I would get the chance to follow the strings to whomever or whatever was holding them. I packed the weapons and the book on the Rejected Enochians by Windham and drove my car to a motel outside the city, where I hoped no one would find me.

Well, no one but Devereaux. A nondescript blue sedan followed me to the motel. The car was so nondescript that it just screamed cop. I didn't try to lose it, because the cops wanted to know where I was going to be. Besides, someone had tried to kill me, so having a police escort wasn't that bad of a deal. I needed to be able to sleep.

9

Later that morning I awoke surprisingly well rested. My entire body felt sore, due to the concussive effect of the grenade, but otherwise I was fine. Devereaux had said that James Williams was in town, so I decided I needed to visit him. Hell, it was quite possible that one of his grenades almost killed me. I needed to meet the man. As to how to find him, well, I knew he'd stay in luxury.

I left my motel room with phone book in hand, checking to make sure that Devereaux's officer pulled into place behind my car as I pulled out of the motel parking lot. Smiling, I drove toward a nearby convenience store parking lot where, after acquiring necessary caffeine, I began calling local hotels. I started at the most expensive and worked my way down the list. James Williams, head of the Sons of Earth group, had checked into the Bourbon Street Fontainebleau Hotel last week. I pulled out of the parking lot and headed downtown. My shadow followed.

The Fontainebleau stood a few stories higher than the older buildings surrounding it. During Mardi Gras, rooms rented for more money per night than most Louisianans made in a month. Few locals would stay there, but with its preeminent location for Mardi Gras, the hotel pulled the rich like a magnet. As I walked in the front door, I saw the Canal Street grandstands built for the parades. On Monday, President Gamble and his entourage would watch the parade from a stand like that one. Was he really in danger? I leaned toward the possibility that Dingo had told at least part of the truth to me, just based on other peoples' reactions to his visit to my emergency room. Anger and grief mixed as I gazed around the Fontainebleau lobby.

Huge chandeliers hung from the two-story ceiling. I figured most of them came from the old houses abandoned near the French Quarter. A middle-aged woman stood behind a mahogany counter. She wore a navy blazer with a white blouse underneath. Her hair showed streaks of gray mixed throughout the brown. She glanced up and smiled as I approached.

"James Williams's suite, please," I said.

The desk clerk looked surprised. "One minute, sir." If nothing else, people in New Orleans kept their courtesy, one of the reasons why I came back here after the War. She picked up the phone. "May I say who's calling?"

"Tell him Captain Roger Stimson is here to pay his respects," I said, trying to keep sarcasm out of my voice. I'm not sure I succeeded.

The desk clerk nodded and dialed. I watched her fingers as they punched the numbers. "Yes, this is Marlissa, the desk attendant," she said. "There's a Captain Roger Stimson here to see Mr. Williams." She pursed out her lips and waited. After a moment, she said, "Thank you, sir." She hung up the phone.

"Captain Stimson, Mr. Williams is not expecting you," she said. "He will not be seeing you, sir. I'm sorry." She looked as if she had told me that I didn't have long to live, which I assumed was true if Williams had his way.

"Thanks for trying," I said. I walked away before she said anything else. A man stood by the elevators, not watching me with interest. I rounded a corner and stopped.

He almost ran into me. "I'm sorry," he said and continued walking toward a sitting area. He grabbed one of the papers and resumed not watching.

I glanced around the corner. The desk clerk was helping another guest, so I decided to try the elevator. I just hoped I had seen the right numbers. The elevator opened and I stepped on after an older couple stepped off. The man smiled and nodded. I smiled back. As the doors closed, the man not watching me tried to catch the door, but failed, almost losing a finger in the process.

I stood in front of the door, wondering about my best course of action. I thought about kicking the door off its hinges, but that would warn the guards and I'd probably get shot. If I did live or if I had the wrong room, then the police would arrive and Devereaux would get his chance in that backroom with the rubber hose. I knocked on the door.

The spyglass went dark and I heard the lock disengaged. The door opened wide, but a man, a big man, filled the doorway. He glared, meaning to intimidate me into leaving. I noticed the bulge under his suit coat. He grinned. I knew I had the correct room.

"No reporters," he said, the voice a tad too high for his body.

"I'm not a reporter," I said. "Tell James Williams that Roger Stimson is here, and that I will see him one way or another."

"Get lost," the big man said, as he stepped back to slam the door in my face. He never got the chance.

My right foot shot to his knee with enough force to buckle his legs. He hit the floor, but rolled to retrieve his gun. Another kick popped him in the face and he plopped onto his back, groaning.

"What in the hell?" A second bodyguard ran from another room in the suite. He pulled his pistol and aimed it at me. "I will kill you." He glanced at his partner.

"I have no doubt that you'll kill me," I followed his eyes. "He'll be all right, but he's gonna have a hell of a headache and probably a broken nose, not to mention a sore knee."

"Captain Roger Stimson," said a man standing behind the other bodyguard. Williams walked to the side of the man pointing the weapon. He was about my age, fortyish, but with long hair and a well-trimmed beard. His eyes held the fire of obsession, as if only he had the truth. "It's okay, Blake. Put the gun away and go help Ladner. Captain Stimson went to a lot of trouble to meet with me. I doubt he will try anything."

The bodyguard hesitated, but complied. He stared at me as he walked to his partner. Williams pointed to the patio door. "It's a beautiful day, Captain," he said. "Shall we sit on the balcony?" He led the way, but stopped as I passed him. "Blake, bring some coffee when you get through."

"Yes, sir," Blake said as he assisted his partner to his feet. The other bodyguard limped to a chair and rubbed his knee. I saw my shoe's imprint on his cheek. He glared at me and touched his gun, but did not draw it. I grinned.

It was cold for New Orleans, but I followed Williams outside. A north wind slapped my face as I stood on the balcony. Williams walked to the railing and stared at the people milling around below.

"I love Mardi Gras," Williams said without turning to me. "It's so explosive."

"Speaking of explosives, I believe one of yours blew up my apartment last night," I said.

Williams turned, a frown formed on his face. "I'm afraid you may be correct, Captain," he said. "One of our, uh, storage areas was burglarized a few nights ago. My guard said he thought he saw a damn Enochian."

I would have thought he would deny the accusation, so

his candor caught me off-guard. I started to ask a question, but Blake brought the coffee outside and placed it on a metal table and left with a wary glance my way.

Williams pointed toward the chairs and I sat. He poured the coffee. "Sugar or cream?"

"I'll take it black," I said. I sipped, savoring the chicory. "An Enochian delivered your 'supplies' to my apartment last night—a fragmenting grenade, as a matter of fact." I took another sip of the coffee, which appeared to be helping against the cold. "Since when does the Sons of Earth work with the Lanaka?"

His eyes lost their hospitality. "We never work with animals," he said. "If an Enochian tried to kill you, then I assure you we had nothing to do with it." Williams's smile returned. I knew he was lying. "Besides, you've proven yourself quite resourceful, Captain. Today, as well as when you released that virus on the aliens."

I put the cup on the table and stood over him. I wanted to wipe the smirk off his face. "If I find that you had anything to do with killing my coworkers and trying to kill me, I will be back." I walked away.

Inside, both bodyguards stood between the door and me, each holding a .38 pointing in my general direction. I stopped and thought about my first move. Blake looked nervous. Obviously, the other one, Ladner, was the badass of the two and I had beat the shit out him, as evidenced by his left eye being swollen shut. Of course, I knew that whichever I attacked first, the other one would shoot me before I could get the .45 out of my jacket.

"Captain, I am quite sorry to hear about the deaths of your friends, a tragedy to be sure," Williams said as he followed me inside. "What about that alien in your emergency room?"

I didn't take my eyes off the bodyguards. "What about him?"

"Did you believe his outrageous tale?"

"Everyone who came in contact with him is dead," I said. "I think there may be something to his story." I glanced over my shoulder and noticed Williams holding another weapon aimed at me.

"You should know that a New Orleans cop is waiting for me in the lobby, probably pretty damn worried that I slipped by him," I said. "I'm sure he already knows that you're staying here. He'll put two and two together in a few minutes."

Williams smiled. "You may leave, Captain." Williams nodded at the bodyguards, who holstered their weapons. As I reached the door, Williams said, "I think it may be you who are working with the Lanaka, Captain."

"I'm not working with anybody," I said. "And I'm not a captain. I'm a nurse." I slammed the door as I left.

When the elevator doors closed, I pressed the button for the lobby and leaned against the elevator's sidewall, shaking. The man not watching me appeared relieved when the doors opened in the lobby. He studiously avoided my eyes as I walked onto Bourbon Street. Making my way toward the French Quarter, I thought about what Williams said. Maybe I was working for the Lanaka. I shook my head. *Too late to worry about that now,* I thought as I went to meet the fake Secret Service agent.

I arrived in Jackson Square for my meeting with Barnett an hour and a half early. If someone were planning a trap for me, the trap would already be waiting. I stood in the doorway of the St. Louis Cathedral and looked across at the famous coffeehouse where Barnett, the fake Secret Service agent, had told me to meet her. I glanced to my left to see if Devereaux's policeman had continued his not-watching of me. The man was eating one of the Café Du Monde beignets with a cup of the chicory coffee that the natives love so much.

I turned away and smiled at the irony of the cop and the doughnut. *Cops and doughnuts are so stereotypical,* I thought, *but I never remembered hearing of a donut shop being robbed.*

I was only blocks from where President Gamble was supposed to be observing the first of the many Mardi Gras parades this coming Monday. *Jackson Square will be packed that day,* I thought as I noticed that a pretty good crowd was milling around the Square for an early Friday afternoon. A street musician was setting up his area, where he would be playing the horn for the night. Groups of people were walking by the cathedral, gazing at the old structure, trying to get a feel for how old the city of New Orleans really was.

Even in the dead of winter on a forty-two-degree day, you could smell the ancientness of the city. New Orleans was a city that had lived hard for the last couple hundred or so years, and parts of it looked it. The horn player had begun playing when I spotted Barnett.

She smiled at the street musician, dropped a dollar in his horn case, and kept on walking. I leaned back into the shadows of the cathedral to watch her. She didn't notice me as she walked around the square, looking and laughing. Barnett looked like a tourist at play, much different from the cold young woman who had questioned me with her murderous Enochian friend. She walked around the Square toward the Café Du Monde. Stopping, she glanced around in the same manner in which she had made a quick danger assessment inside my apartment. Satisfied, she continued past the Café Du Monde to the levee.

My friends who grew up here all tell me that it is an optical illusion, but New Orleans is the only place in the world that I have had to walk uphill to get to the water level of the Mississippi River. If the levee was not in place, I'm sure the Old River would inundate the Café Du Monde, St. Louis Cathedral, and all of the other famous tourist traps the city offers to visitors.

Barnett stopped and sat on a bench facing the river, her back to me. I watched her for a few minutes to make sure that she was alone. Several groups of people moved past her as I watched, but after ten minutes, no one had stopped. "Well, we'll just have our meeting an hour or so early, Miss Barnett, or whoever the hell you are," I mumbled to myself. An old drunk sitting opposite me in the doorway looked up, and then dropped his head back to his chest.

I walked out of the cathedral and headed toward the river. I felt, rather than saw, that my police shadow had moved into step, a little behind me. Away from the cathedral entrance, I felt the cold, swirling wind, so I wrapped my coat a little tighter around me. I felt the reassuring touch of my .45 in the inside pocket of the coat. The wind shifted slightly, bringing with it the smell of the pastries and the chicory flavor of the coffee. It had been years since I had been to the Café Du Monde. *Maybe later,* I thought. Barnett had not moved from her seat as I passed the Café and went to the walkway that led to the levee. I lost sight of her as I wound my way to the top. When I reached the levee walkway, I breathed a sigh of relief. Barnett was still there.

I walked up behind her. She did not turn around. A chill went through my chest that had nothing to do with the cold weather. I had seen it too many times not to recognize the symptoms. Barnett was not breathing. I noticed that her head bent slightly toward the river.

"Oh, shit," I said, running to the bench. I knelt in front of her as cold, blue eyes stared at me. The pupils were fixed and dilated. A small amount of blood oozed from the left corner of her mouth. I reached up to grab her shoulder to shake her and she fell into my arms. I lowered her to the ground, ignoring the blood that soaked my own clothes. Something hard fell against my hand and I picked it up and moved it before I saw that the object was a gun.

Looking around, I saw a broad-shouldered figure walking toward the river.

"Hey, stop you son of a bitch." The alien turned to look at me. I got up from the body and took three steps toward the Enochian when I heard my shadow hollering.

"Stimson, stop your ass, right there," the cop said. I heard the click of a hammer being pulled back, ready to fire. I stopped. Rafta, the midget alien, bent his knees and jumped down from the levee and then to the roof of a nearby building. "Holy shit," the cop said.

I turned around to look, when something hit me hard and knocked the breath out of me. The next thing I knew I seemed to be flying through the air, gasping for breath, with a blue arm around my waist. Glass shattered as my abductor and I went through a closed window. Something hit the back of my head and I lost consciousness.

PART TWO

DINGO RUN

PROLOG

Breaking news reports on the Los Angeles massacre.

The announcer puts a hand to his ear.

Announcer: We've got breaking news. Reports are coming in that a large explosion has devastated the Greater Los Angeles area. Alien ships had been sighted in the vicinity of the blast. What? We have reporters on their way to the scene.

A woman walks in from the left and lays a paper on the announcer's desk. He reads, leaving the air quiet for a minute. He looks up. His eyebrows are scrunched up and he appears to be having trouble talking.

Announcer: The United States government is now confirming that Los Angeles has been attacked by alien forces. I quote: "Southern California was devastated by an Enochian spaceship today. Casualty estimates will be extremely heavy, as the attack centered on Los Angeles. As many as one million people may be dead in the attack."

The announcer stops reading and listens as a producer talks in his ear.

Announcer: Oh my God, can that be correct? Somebody double-check that, please? You're saying this is confirmed information.

Announcer stares into camera.

Announcer: Please excuse me for a moment. *He rubs his eyes and stares at his desk.* I'm sorry. This is a shocking

71

story. I don't care who you are, you have to be affected by the extreme loss of life. I'm being told that the Enochians are claiming that the explosion was an accident. We'll stay right here as this horrible story develops.

10

I awoke, but kept my eyes closed, as I could hear the clicks and whistles of the Enochian language. The alien seemed to be talking to himself. I rolled over and felt for my .45. It was not in my jacket. Either it fell out during my abduction or the alien had taken it off me. I moved my left ankle and could feel the .32 loaned to me by Devereaux. Feeling a little better, I half opened my eyes. The clicking and whistling continued, as I saw an Enochian pounding away at an ordinary personal computer.

I closed my eyes and listened to the quality of the alien language being used. I heard a lot of the language during the War. This was not the pleading sound I heard from many of our test subjects in the Bio-Chem lab. This was an angry clicking that a few of the most desperate, the ones who had not resigned themselves to our manipulations of their genetic code, the ones who had not resigned themselves to death, had made. They were the dangerous ones, our group had concluded. Even though I considered my life in danger, I could not help but feel the irony that I, the man who gave the recommendation to use the virus against the aliens, and actually released the virus, might die at the hands of an Enochian.

Wham!

I jumped at the sound of the alien slamming his hand on the computer desk. I opened my eyes and reached for the small-caliber pistol in the leg holster, swinging myself up in one move. I aimed the weapon at the alien's most vulnerable spot, the back of the neck just below the skull. If I was going to die, I was going to hurt the son of a bitch before he killed me. The Enochian turned around to look at me.

He ignored my gun and spoke. "Do you know anything about computers?" He had turned around to face me. I noticed the tattoo on his chest, below where nipples would have been on a human. I half-grinned at the sight of the happy face in red ink on the blue skin. I re-aimed the weapon to the equator of the exploding Earth.

"Hello, Dingo," I said as calmly as I could. "I've been looking for you." Dingo clicked at me. I shrugged, indicating that I did not understand. He seemed to notice the gun aimed at him for the first time and puffed his jowls, I assumed as a shrug.

"You better be a damn good shot," he said, "because if you're not, then that little thing is just going to piss me off."

I blinked and must have looked surprised at his comment. Dingo laughed. I thought about what he said. A .32 doesn't carry a big punch. During the War, we noticed that .50-caliber weapons only slowed down an assault, unless loaded with armor-piercing bullets. The thick skin and even thicker bones made marksmanship a necessity to hit the vulnerable areas of an Enochian. I had not kept practice with my shooting, but I didn't lower the gun. There were too many variables here.

Dingo sighed. "Look," he said. "The same people who are trying to kill you are trying to kill me. And we both know why, don't we, Captain Stimson?"

No one had called me "Captain" since the War, and now both Boudreau and Dingo had reminded me of my military rank in the last two days. *How does he know about me?* I wondered. My thoughts crept back to the virus. *Does he know what I did?*

Dingo interrupted my reverie. "We really are on the same side." Dingo kept his eyes on me, but did not move, keeping still. Regardless of whether it would kill him, the alien had enough sense to know that a gunshot wound would still hurt. I laid the gun down. Dingo relaxed, letting out a long breath. "Good," he said. "Now, do you know anything about computers?"

"What are you trying to do?" I walked over to the PC console and peered at the screen. I laughed, because Dingo was trying to break into Secret Service files. "You know our government can trace your hacking attempt."

"No, they can't," he replied. I started to protest, but he held up a four-fingered hand. "Trust me; they can't trace it, at least not to this location." He laughed, I guess because of the look on my face.

"Computers, I can use, but hacking my way into secure servers is not one of my strengths," I said. "What are you trying to get into?"

"Too bad. I need to know if the Secret Service is taking the threat to Gamble's life seriously."

"They take *every* threat to a President's life seriously," I said, speaking from historical assurance, even though I knew from my meeting with Allen that they weren't taking *this* threat seriously.

Dingo puffed his jowls. "Did they come see you? Did they contact that NOPD detective who is investigating the murders of your workmates?" He puffed one more time and continued. "I'm sure they did, but it doesn't matter." Dingo pushed away from the computer and stared at the screen. "No, Captain Stimson, I'm afraid that everything is going according to schedule and Gamble will be here Monday morning to watch the first parade." Dingo stopped talking and sighed.

"You really believe that someone will try to kill Gamble?" I knew the answer to my question, and I knew what Dingo had said a couple of nights ago. I thought of all the people killed because of his visit to the emergency room. I believed it.

"No, I don't believe; I know," he said with an air of certainty. "And it's up to us to stop it."

"Why can't you just go to the authorities?" I wondered if Dingo was on Earth without our government's knowledge.

"There would be . . ." Dingo hesitated, as if choosing his words carefully, ". . . complications. Besides, they would not believe a drunkard alien with a story like this. No, it's up to you and me, Captain."

Dingo fell silent. I stared at the creature and wondered how he seemed to know so much about me, but I wasn't ready to ask that question yet. I cleared my throat. "If you're so sure—"

Dingo exploded. "How can you doubt all the evidence you've seen? Everyone who has come into contact with me is dead. That should tell you that something is up."

His anger startled me. I pulled the gun back out and aimed it at Dingo again.

"Put that thing away," he said, waving his hand as if dismissing the gun's importance. He puffed twice, and I saw that he had calmed himself somewhat.

I did as he asked. "Dingo, don't do that," I said, admonishing him. "If you want my trust—and I don't trust most *people,* much less a six-five alien whose species tried to exterminate my species—then you are going about this the wrong way."

Be damned if he didn't look confused. When he spoke, his voice showed no trace of the anger he had displayed. "I'm not asking you to trust me," he said. "Just look at the facts. I came to your emergency room and shot my drunken mouth off. Within twenty-four hours, everyone is dead except me and you." Dingo stood up and looked down at me. "Do you really believe that all of this is a coincidence? Haven't you wondered how I know you were a captain in

76

the past war between our species?" He looked menacing, towering over me. "Do you think that I, and others like me, do not know what you did in the War?"

Moving with caution, I put the gun in my pocket and stood as straight as I could. "I did my duty," I said, trying to keep the guilt hidden, but it swelled up behind my words.

"And your duty damn near wiped out my species." Dingo sat down, the chair under him strained to the limit. It had not been manufactured with the Enochian in mind. "After the War, the Rejected managed to smuggle the antidote/vaccine to the war party."

My shoulders slumped and I felt the long-held guilt full-force in my abdomen. "It was always my intention to get the antidote to your leaders," I said with the frustration and anger of my impotence forcing its way into the next words I spoke. "But the damn generals and politicians nixed the plan. After your ships left our system, I smuggled the antidote, and instructions on how to manufacture more of it, to the ones left behind, the Rejects like you."

We were quiet, each reflecting on our personal tragedies. Finally, I said, "I'm glad it made it back to your home planet."

"Even then, it was almost too late," Dingo said. He looked up at me and gave me the smile I had seen when he was drunk in the ER. "But, Stimson, we do not hold grudges. We learned an immense amount about you and ourselves as a result. In the long run, the experience has strengthened my people.

"But enough of the past; we have problems for the present," Dingo said, turning back to the computer.

But I wasn't through.

11

We were quiet for a few moments. Dingo punched away at the computer, cussing in Enochian, while I glanced around the room. Tasteful furniture occupied the large room, with the computer system on one side of the room and a huge fireplace on the other. I could see a large kitchen across the way. An open banister delineated the second floor, about halfway up the wall beneath the cathedral ceilings. This house was expensive. Whatever Dingo was, he was extremely well-financed.

"Where the hell are we?" I asked.

Dingo didn't stop with his work on breaking into the Secret Service computers, but answered me. "This is my house," he said without taking his attention from the computer screen.

I looked around and whistled, thinking I had misjudged the alien. I had to ask. "If this is your house, then what the hell were you doing living under a bridge? I would think you would enjoy your whiskey a lot better here."

Dingo stopped working with a shrill whistle and forceful click. "I can't get in, but I think we have to assume that Gamble will be present for the Mardi Gras parades on Monday." He looked at me. "Did you ask me something?"

"I asked what you were doing under that bridge near the old airport, living with the bums, when you have a house like this. And by the way, how—"

Dingo interrupted me. "One question at a time, please," he said. "I enjoy the drinking, as you no doubt know all of my people do. It's amazing that we never discovered the pleasures of whiskey. I guess it's because we don't have corn to ferment." Dingo smiled, a whimsical look on his face.

I sighed and shook my head. "That doesn't explain why you were with the bums, playing troll."

Dingo looked at me intently. "You can learn a lot about a culture by studying its rejects, those that are not a part of the societal whole," he said. "Your own government understood that. That's why they financed that anthropologist in New Mexico."

I figured he was talking about Windham, but I didn't correct him that she was from Texas. It would only mean something to Texans, not Enochians. "How did you come by this house?"

Dingo quit smiling. "I have my resources."

A thought came into my head. "You're selling technology," I said. "You're selling Enochian technology."

Dingo puffed his jowls, but said nothing.

He's not going to admit it, I thought, and changed the subject. "What do your neighbors think of having an Enochian neighbor?"

"They don't know," he said. "They've never seen me." I noticed the newspaper lying on the computer desk. Dingo glanced down and picked up the paper. "I pay my carrier an extra ten dollars a month to slide it through the mail slot." He opened the front page. "You need to look at this, by the way."

He handed the paper to me. My picture and name were on the top of the front page. Next to it was a picture of Devereaux, who was quoted as saying that I was the main suspect in a number of murders over the last couple of days. The good detective neglected to mention that he himself had loaned me a gun.

"I didn't kill anyone," I said, anger in my voice. "How dare they accuse me of murder? I guess I blew up my own apartment." I looked over the paper at Dingo.

"I know," Dingo said. "However, Captain Stimson, you were seen with the murder weapon on the Riverwalk." He looked me up and down. "And I suspect that the blood on your shirt is from the victim, one Valerie Barnett. She was a high-echelon member in the Sons of Earth movement." Dingo watched for my reaction.

I tried to keep a blank look on my face. Considering the stress I was under, it was easy.

"Captain, the only way you can clear yourself is to help me stop this assassination." Dingo sighed and puffed. "I rather think that no one will believe any story you give, either, after that," he said, indicating the newspaper.

I threw the paper on the couch. "All right," I said, resigned to the fact that I was stuck with the alien. "Where do we start? And how do you know about my military record?"

Dingo whistled and clucked. "We start by getting on the Enochian Reservation. I'm not sure how the hell to do that, because I'm not exactly welcome." Dingo hesitated. "If we do get in, we may have trouble getting you out. I'm not the only one who knows your background." I nodded.

"As to how I know about your background," the alien continued, "Bilbro told me."

"Who's Bilbro?"

"An Enochian agent of the Lanaka," the alien said, with no particular emotion. "The Lanaka kept a presence on your world, clandestinely; not a large presence, but a presence. That's how the virus antidote made it back to the homeworld."

My mouth fell open. Dingo studied me as he let the information sink in. The Lanaka had stayed behind. Why?

To monitor us? Or to monitor the Rejects? I closed my mouth.

"You didn't come to my emergency room by accident," I said. It was an accusation.

Dingo showed a most human trait of nodding his head. Enochians just didn't do that, and it looked unnatural for him, but he had picked up many human attributes in his time here.

"The Lanaka knew where you were," Dingo said, quietly. "Bilbro said that if just informing your security forces—which we knew that you would do—did not work, then I needed a backup plan." Dingo laughed again. I think he just liked the sound of his laughter. "You were the backup plan."

"What in hell do you people think I could do?"

"We found that you were a formidable enemy," Dingo said, as if he were teaching a lesson. "Formidable enemies make formidable allies, if they don't kill you first." I took the last to be another reference to my part in the release of the Enochian virus. "Besides, Captain, you owe us." He hesitated, as if deciding how much information to tell me. "Bilbro was not stationed on Earth. He was an advance scout for a trip by the Prefect."

"The Prefect is coming to Earth?" I couldn't believe it. After years of silence, the Enochians were making overtures of peace. *That's presumptuous*, I thought. "Why would he come here after all these years, Dingo?"

"Because, my dear Captain," Dingo said in that same academic tone, "a formidable enemy can become a formidable ally." Dingo puffed. "Gamble may not be the only target for assassination on Monday afternoon. The murder of our Prefect would annihilate your planet. And, as far as I know, the trip is still on," he said. "I can't seem to find Bilbro for confirmation."

I remembered the dead alien lying in the New Orleans City Morgue. "Detective Devereaux called me and asked if I would identify a dead Enochian," I said. "I thought it might be you. It wasn't."

"Obviously," he said. "And it obviously wasn't the short, stubby bastard running around killing humans indiscriminately. That has got to stop." Dingo stroked his left jowl, thinking. "I've got to get a look at that body."

"Why?"

Dingo looked surprised by my question. "For one reason, to confirm or deny that it is Bilbro." Dingo sighed. "And to see how he was killed. It could have been a ritual murder."

"Are you a pathologist, or whatever you guys have that studies dead aliens?"

Dingo rose what on a human would have been an eyebrow, another human gesture. "I'm the closest thing on Earth to one."

I couldn't argue with his logic. "And just how do you plan on getting into the morgue to see that body?" A few dozen cops worked just above the morgue, one of whom was my friend Devereaux, who wanted to throw my ass in jail.

The alien laughed. "Why, you're going to turn yourself in, of course." Dingo laughed again.

I didn't find the idea of being charged with multiple murders that amusing. I frowned and looked down at my shirt. "Have you got a place I can clean up? I'd rather not give up with my supposed victim's blood covering the front of my shirt."

12

Devereaux was waiting out front, when we arrived at the morgue. We had taken Dingo's truck because of the dark-tinted windows and the fact that it was the only vehicle big enough for him and available to us. Devereaux was dressed in the same bulky suit he had been wearing yesterday morning. I wondered if he ever slept, or did he live his job, as many people in our types of services do. We parked in front of the building.

"I'm glad you called me and decided to turn yourself in, Stimson," the detective said as I was getting out of the truck. He opened his mouth to say something else, but the words caught in his throat as Dingo got out of the other door. The alien walked around the car to stand beside us, towering over Devereaux, who looked up at the Enochian in disbelief.

"Detective Devereaux, I want you to meet Dingo," I said nonchalantly. "He also happens to be an eyewitness to the killing of Valerie Barnett."

Devereaux stuck out his hand, which Dingo grabbed in response. "I've heard a lot about you," Devereaux said, looking up at Dingo.

"And I know a lot about you, Detective."

Dingo's statement did not go unnoticed by Devereaux, who blinked, glanced at me, and waved us inside. It was good to get out of the open. I'd had too many potshots taken at me in the last thirty-six hours.

The building was on skeletal crew, due to the early hour

on a Saturday morning. We saw one security guard as we went toward the morgue. I had told Devereaux over the phone that the only way I would give up was if he would allow me to see the alien's body again. He had agreed, somewhat reluctantly. He didn't wait long to question me about the killing at Jackson Square on the river.

"Why were you following Ms. Barnett?" Devereaux kept his eyes forward as he walked.

"Because she had introduced herself to me as Valerie Barnett, Secret Service agent, and had credentials to prove it," I said. "She called me and asked for a meeting. I knew it might be a setup, and I knew that you would have me followed. As a matter of fact, I made damn sure your officer would not lose me yesterday morning. He was pretty good at not watching me."

Devereaux nodded.

We stopped at the elevator and waited. The detective turned to Dingo. "And you're the one who started this entire ruckus by claiming that someone was going to kill the President."

Dingo puffed his jowls. "Detective, I expected more from you. Your records indicate that you are a free thinker, with an excellent investigative technique. Use your brain and tell me if what I claim is true."

Devereaux turned red in the face. I made a mental note to thank Dingo for pissing off the detective who was probably going to arrest me for murder, but Devereaux did not explode. Instead, the elevator doors opened and we rode in silence to the basement where the bodies were kept. The manner in which Devereaux was handling this matter confused me. I expected to be cuffed and bundled off to some unknown precinct, and harassed to give a confession; however, the detective surprised me. He kept his silence and, when the elevator opened, slowly led us down the hall toward the morgue. I began to get uneasy. Dingo was wearing his best "I'm just a drunkard old alien" face. He looked as though he were somewhat enjoying the whole process.

Devereaux stopped a few feet from the door to the morgue and grabbed both of us by the arms for us to stop too. I didn't see him pull his pistol, but it was in his hand as he motioned to us to stay back, while he went to the door, five feet in front of us. Dingo and I pressed against the wall and crept up behind him. The detective crouched, slightly, as he flung open the door.

"Hold it right there," Devereaux screamed.

I could hear the clatter of metal hitting the floor and a human voice hollering back at the detective, "Don't shoot. Please, don't shoot." Devereaux's body was taut, including his ample rounded gut, but his aim did not waver. I realized that I was holding my breath. After a few agonizing seconds, I could see Devereaux straighten and relax. He let his weapon drop to his side. Devereaux laughed. I remembered to breathe.

"I don't think it's too damn funny," said the voice in the other room.

Devereaux laughed louder and turned to us. "Come on," he said to us, grinning. "Let me introduce you to the assistant coroner." His grin got wider. "Don't mind the smell in here; I just scared the shit out of him."

We followed Devereaux into the room. Something was wrong. I could feel it. I looked around, but nothing was out of the ordinary, as far as I could tell. I had been in the room only once before, but I had the sensitivity of a man who had been shot at and blown up recently. I couldn't quite put my finger on it. I looked at Dingo, who had remained tense, much different from his usual countenance. Devereaux appeared unaware of the smell of something wrong.

Smell, I thought, *that's it.* I leaned toward Dingo and said, "An Enochian has been here." Dingo grunted. The alien was not as tall as he had been. I glanced up and down at him and noticed that his knees were flexed, ready for action.

"We want to see the alien," Devereaux said to the assistant.

"That's not possible," the assistant said, nervousness obvious in his voice. "The Secret Service has restricted access to the body."

"What?" Devereaux was incredulous. "They can't do that. That body is part of a goddamn murder investigation." The detective stopped and seemed to sniff the air. "Oh," I heard him say, whispering to himself.

Devereaux had never holstered his weapon, so he brought it up to his shoulder, holding the gun in both hands. The detective looked around the morgue warily. The assistant screamed, "Get down!" A red dot appeared in the middle of his forehead before he could follow his own advice. I knew he was dead before he hit the floor.

All hell broke loose.

A blue streak went by me. I heard the crash of Dingo's head hitting the wall from his leap. I hit the ground and pulled Devereaux's borrowed gun from the ankle holster I was wearing.

Bullets flew past my ears as I scrambled to one of the metal exam tables. Hiding behind the table, I pulled the body closer to me. I felt bullets tear into the body's cold, bluish flesh. Those bullets were meant for me, which of course irritated me to no end. As far as I could figure, there were at least three gunmen in the morgue, and they were firing from an alcove behind the door. One of the shooters ran for the door, firing just to keep our heads down.

I aimed and fired. The shooter went down and did not move. I saw something blue streak toward the table I was hiding behind.

The next thing I knew, both the table and the corpse were on top of me. I heard the door to the morgue open and the sound of footsteps running down the hall. I got my head out from under the body on top of me and saw an Enochian standing over me with a gun pointed at my forehead. It was Rafta. The alien said nothing. I heard two loud gunshots from my left and saw Rafta stagger back. The alien tucked his legs under him and jumped through the door of the morgue. His heavier footsteps followed the same path as his partner.

The body on top of me was heavy. It was only then that I noticed that it was the Enochian I had misidentified on purpose the day before. I pushed my way out from underneath the corpse and swung around to my left as I heard a noise.

"What have I told you about pointing that little thing at me?" I brought my aim off Dingo, who walked over and looked at the dead Enochian. "Yeah, that's Bilbro." Dingo puffed. "Damn it." The Enochian clicked and whistled the rest of his curses.

I got up and looked around the room. I found the morgue assistant first. Right beside him, I saw Devereaux lying face-down. Blood pooled around the detective's head, but I could not tell if it came from his wounds.

"Come on," Dingo said. "Let's get out of here. With him dead, the NOPD is going to think you did it. You are still wanted for murder, Stimson, and we can't be slowed down by you being in jail." He grabbed my jacket and pulled me away from Devereaux. I never got to take a pulse, and I couldn't tell if the detective was breathing. "We've got to go," Dingo said, insisting that I follow him by pulling on my jacket.

We ran out of the morgue and up the stairs. The lone guard had a sucking chest wound, which hissed at us as we ran past him and through the door. I wanted to stop and help, but Dingo pulled me toward the truck. Sirens wailed in the distance as Dingo pulled away from the morgue building. We hit I-10 and headed west. I didn't ask where we were going. I had to trust that Dingo knew what he was doing.

I looked at the alien in the early light of dawn, as we were leaving New Orleans. "Brush the plaster off your head," I told him. Somewhere in the bullet-ridden morgue was a hole in a wall about the size of Dingo's head. We drove west in silence.

13

We were just coming out of Lake Charles when I awoke. The sun was fairly high in the sky, and Dingo was driving about ninety in a seventy-mile-per-hour speed zone and talking on a cell phone. I stayed still and listened as he talked.

"Yeah, I want it in Beaumont," the alien said, sounding as human as I. "Just leave the keys inside and have it gassed up, then come back after the truck later." He paused. "Okay, then, we'll be there in about an hour. Yeah. Thanks." He punched the off-button and put the phone back into his coat pocket. I felt a hand grab my shoulder.

"Hey, Stimson," he said as he pulled me upright. "You do know that your breathing changes when you're awake, don't you?"

I stretched and yawned before I responded. I wanted a cigarette for the first time in years. *Stress and nicotine seem to go together,* I thought. A couple of large oil refineries lined both sides of Interstate 10 as we sped by. I had always been fascinated by the fires coming out of the pipes. I remembered coming over the Lake Charles I-10 bridge at night, and all you could see were lights flowing to the horizon on both sides, like Christmas all year long.

"Don't you think you ought to slow down?" I asked, pointing at the speedometer. "We don't know that this truck wasn't seen as we left New Orleans. Besides, it'll be tough enough to explain an alien to the Louisiana Highway Patrol."

"No cops around with that primitive radar you guys have," Dingo said, puffing. "And this is slow enough. Once we get out of this traffic, I'll speed up a bit."

I grunted. Enochian reflexes are quite a bit faster than ours are. I wondered how big their bladders were. "I forget if you guys have to urinate or not," I said, sitting up as straight as I could to relieve the pressure on my bladder. "But unless you want the leather seats on your truck wet, you better find a place for me to pee."

"Yes, we do urinate, though not as often as I found that humans do," Dingo said, with no humor or accusation. It was true enough that the aliens were bigger in most respects than humans were. I thought back to the other night, when he came into the emergency room and we undressed him to check for any other injuries. If he stopped at a roadside with a communal trough, there were going to be some envious males.

Dingo pulled into a rest stop a few miles before the Texas state line. We got out of the truck and walked to the bathroom. I couldn't help but notice that all eyes were on my companion as we walked. *The cops will not have a hard time tracing our path,* I thought.

The urinals were not communal troughs, but individual stations with a small wall between each for a minimum of privacy, and I do mean a minimum of privacy. Dingo walked into a stall anyway. I could hear a couple of the people in the bathroom whispering, until what sounded like a high-pressure hose was unleashed in Dingo's stall. Muffled laughter mixed in with the sound of Niagara. I finished and turned to walk to the sink to wash my hands.

Two country boys stood in my way, and neither of them were amused. Both had guts from too many years of beer and not enough years of exercise. One was about my height and had a mound of what I took to be tobacco bulging out of one side of his mouth. Brown spit oozed out of the left corner of his mouth and mingled with a scraggly grayish beard. He looked disgusting, like many of the hard-asses who tramped through my ER.

"Why'n you travelin' with that goddamn animal for, boy," Tobacco Breath said as he smiled. I realized that he was not chewing the cud in his mouth. He couldn't chew it. He was at a deficit of teeth in the tooth-to-tattoo ratio. His somewhat shorter, but no smaller, buddy smiled, too. The shorter one had a couple of teeth up front. I wondered if that was because he didn't chew tobacco. I tried to move past them, but Tobacco Breath grabbed my arm. "I'm talkin' to you, boy."

"Get your hands off of me, sir," I said quietly, while looking him in the eyes. Tobacco Breath did not let go. Other people in the washroom left in a hurry, and some that came in decided they would wait until reaching the Texas state line about twenty miles down the road. Tobacco Breath increased his grip on my arm.

"I fought to kill those sons a bitches," he said, spitting tobacco juice over my face, "and here you is ridin' with one."

"Hey, leave him alone," Dingo said. I had heard the pressure hose disconnect, with Niagara drying up, and expected him out any moment.

Tobacco Breath turned his head slightly, as did his friend. At the same time, I jumped back out of his grasp and, before he could turn around to face me, I laid an elbow against the side of his head. Tobacco Breath was down before his friend knew what to do. The friend looked around and found a second elbow in both of his nostrils. He fell on top of Tobacco Breath.

Dingo came out of the stall, looked at the two men on the rest area floor, and puffed. "I can't take you anywhere." He walked out of the bathroom and strolled back to the car. I followed, and we left before the cops got there. Tobacco Breath and his friend weren't going to be bothering anyone for a little while.

Dingo hit the interstate at seventy and cruised up to eighty-five before setting the cruise control. He stroked a jowl and glanced at me sideways. "Where did you learn to fight?"

"Left over from the military," I said. "It's one of the few things from those days that I've kept up with. Comes in quite handy in the emergency room."

"Hmm," Dingo said. "I'll bet."

I changed the subject. "Who are we meeting in Beaumont?"

"No one," Dingo said, cheerfully. He didn't elaborate.

I sighed. "I heard the phone call; you know I heard," I said, anger returning to my voice. I was tired of being left out of the information loop. "It's time we quit playing games with each other, and you need to start telling me the truth."

Dingo laughed. I fumed in quiet for the next twenty miles. After we went over the Sabine River into Texas, I broached the subject again with a little less anger this time. The adrenaline from the roadside fight had worn off as the Texas landscape flew past the window. It didn't look much different from Louisiana.

"We're going to the Beaumont airport and picking up a plane," Dingo said. "Eighty-five will not get us where we need to be in the little time we have to get there."

"What did you say?" I furrowed my brow and stared open-mouthed for a moment. Dingo grinned. "Never mind," I said.

He reached into the back seat, pulled out a small case, and handed it to me. "Hit the Net and find out where the anthropologist Denise Windham lives, will you?"

I opened the case and saw a top-of-the-line laptop. "This have built-in wireless capabilities?"

"Yeah," Dingo said. "Only it's not cellular. It picks up the nearest geosynchronous satellites."

"Interesting," I said. Punching the buttons, I hit the Net in no time. The damn hand-held was more powerful than the models presently on sale. One thing was for sure, Dingo had money. He also had some influence with someone, because this version of the laptop was not yet available to the public.

"Oh, I get it," I said, as a little light flashed in my head. I looked at Dingo and smiled. "You're not selling to the government, or at least not entirely."

Dingo puffed at me. "Are you going to get that address?"

I wondered if selling his species' technological secrets might be bothering him a bit. "Selling Enochian technology pays well, does it?"

Dingo ignored my question and changed the subject. "Look for her in New Mexico."

I shook my head. "According to the book I read, she lives in Midland, Texas, and teaches at the University in Odessa." I punched in the data for the Midland city directory. "Why do you want to see her?"

"I've told you," he said. "Windham can get us onto the Enochian Reservation. I, myself, am not very welcome there."

I shook my head, but didn't look up. "All you told me was that we needed to get to the reservation," I said as I searched. "You didn't say anything about Ms. Windham." He didn't answer. "Got it. She lives at 1344 Gulf Avenue."

Dingo disengaged the cruise control and sped the truck up to about ninety-five. I continued to use the computer to search out news databases for anything on a massacre at the New Orleans City Morgue. What I found, I didn't like.

"Dingo, I think I might have a problem going back to work next week," I said. "Devereaux's dead, and my picture is in the news as the leader of the shoot-out in the morgue. There's no mention of Enochians in the story." I read on. "Looks like there is a twenty-thousand-dollar reward for information leading to my capture."

Dingo stroked a jowl. "Twenty thousand, huh? I wonder if there's a bonus for bringing you in alive." The alien laughed and glanced toward me. "I tell you what, Captain. After we stop these assassinations, I'll turn you in and split the money with you." Dingo laughed some more. "Then I'll spring you by being your star witness."

I ignored him and looked for news of the President's visit to Mardi Gras. All seemed to be on target. Hell, the *Times-Picayune* even published the proposed parade route, with exact locations for where Gamble would view the first parade. There was no mention of the Enochian Prefect.

I told Dingo, who I assumed was counting the money that he would get for turning me in. The alien said that the Enochian leader would be in New Orleans. It had already been worked out, according to Bilbro, the dead Lanaka agent. I nodded.

One piece of information that turned up in my search of the news was a small story about the arrest of James Williams, head of the Sons of Earth movement, in New Orleans. The Secret Service released Williams a few hours later. It seems that Williams had given an interview stating that President Gamble should be shot for his attempts at negotiations with the Enochians. I punched up the interview.

A woman's voice asked him a question off-screen. "Mr. Williams, does your organization advocate violence against the Enochian Rejects, who were abandoned by their own people?"

Williams smiled at the interviewer. "We believe that the Enochians should be thrown off Earth and no trace of that God-forsaken race should be left in the universe," Williams said, in a soft, smooth oration. His voice and diction were much different than I thought they should be. I expected him to be closer in kind to the two rednecks I had met outside of Lake Charles. He reminded me more of a good politician, explaining why inflation was eating into the U.S. economy, instead of hinting at the extermination of almost fifteen thousand sentient creatures.

I can't judge him, I thought. *I killed a hell of a lot more Enochians than Williams will get the chance to see in his life.* I noticed that Dingo looked over at the laptop's screen as Williams continued speaking in the interview.

"In fact, I believe that there must be a solution to the humans who want to talk to these spawn of Satan. Do you know how many humans these things killed when they started the War? And I have no doubt that they started the War because—"

I punched the computer button to clear the image of Williams. I'd had enough. Williams, though he probably fought in the War, did not know how many Enochians we killed, ending the War.

"He's dangerous," Dingo said.

I grunted my assent, still thinking about my part in ending the War. "What bothers me is the fact that they took his veiled threat against Gamble seriously enough to arrest him, even if they did release him soon afterward. You and me, they are charging with murder."

"What do you mean *we,* human?" Dingo laughed.

I was getting tired of his humor and turned the computer off. We rode in silence the rest of the way to the Beaumont airport.

The small airport was busy when we got there about noon. Dingo drove to the area reserved for private planes and parked. The alien looked at me and pointed toward a small jet aircraft that was sitting just outside one of the hangers. He got out of the truck and I followed. I knew nothing about airplanes, but I was sufficiently impressed by this one. Dingo opened the door and climbed into the pilot's seat, motioning me around to the other side.

I hesitated. "Do you know how to fly this thing?" I never have liked to fly, and only did it when I had no other choice in the matter.

"I've been flying since I was young," Dingo remarked. "Don't worry, Captain, I'm a safe pilot, even in one of your people's designs."

I got in, but I was still reluctant. The fact that I was wanted for several murders in New Orleans left me no choice.

"Besides, I've made a few changes to the design, based on Enochian technology," Dingo said with a touch of pride in his voice. I thought about how contaminated Dingo had become with his extensive human contact.

I looked at the alien and made a production of buckling my belt. I had not prayed in years, but I seriously considered resuming the practice. Dingo was having too much fun.

Dingo contacted the tower and sounded like every pilot I had ever seen and heard in the movies, requesting clearance to take off. The controllers granted permission, to my dismay, and Dingo taxied onto the runway as we waited for the final clearance to be given. I saw the alien searching in a compartment to his right. "There it is," he said pulling a bottle of whiskey from the compartment.

"You're not going to drink that and fly this plane," I said. It wasn't a question; it was a demand.

Dingo ignored me, unscrewed the top of the bottle, and took a large sip. One-third of the bottle's contents disappeared into his blue gullet. "Ahhh. Haven't had a drink in hours."

I put my face in my hands. "Oh shit," I muttered. "Look, I don't want to fly in this damn thing to begin with, and I sure don't want a drunk pilot." I was livid and more than a bit scared.

Before he could answer me, we were given final clearance. Dingo took another sip and guided the plane down the runway. We were in the air before I knew it. Two more drinks and the whiskey bottle was empty. The alien threw it behind him and fished another one out of the compartment beside him. He seemed to notice me glaring at him.

"Where are my manners?" Dingo handed the bottle to me. I looked down at the ground that was farther away from me every second we flew. I took a long swig of whiskey and swallowed. Now, I really wanted a cigarette. I wanted to tell Dingo to take me back to New Orleans. At least there, I might live a long life in prison, instead of dying in a plane crash with a drunken alien. Dingo finished the bottle as soon as I handed it to him. He fished out a third and took a drink. He punched some buttons on the plane's console and let go of the wheel.

"Now we are on autopilot for the next three hours," he said with a slight slur to his voice. He took another drink and handed me the bottle. I sighed and took another long sip, and a third, before giving it back to Dingo. He punched some more buttons and turned to me. "We'll be at Midland Airport in about three hours. I suggest you get some sleep." He finished the bottle and tossed it behind him. It clinked against the other two. "I know I'm going to. I've programmed the plane to circle over Goldsmith when we get to the Midland area."

"You're going to sleep?"

"Yeah," he said, surprised. "We've got enough fuel to circle for another two hours after we get there, so one of us better wake up in time to land the plane."

"One of us?" I screamed at him. "Dingo, you son of a bitch, I don't know how to fly, much less land this damn thing." He had turned his back to me. "Dingo?" I heard the characteristic snoring of an Enochian asleep. I questioned a lot more than his heritage, which would not have meant much to his people anyway. Human rules don't apply. Leaning back in my seat, I found myself becoming tired. After a while of worrying, I surprised myself and slept.

When I awoke, the aircraft was circling over a bunch of oil pump jacks, which I took to mean that we were at Goldsmith. I checked my watch and found that we had been flying for four hours. I guessed that we had another hour of fuel left. I punched the alien in the shoulder, which hurt my hand and did not stir the Enochian.

"Dingo," I said, shaking him. "Wake up. We're circling and we only have an hour of fuel left."

Dingo responded groggily. "Punch the red button," he said with a slur. "It'll land us in Midland."

"No," I said in a controlled voice. "You wake your blue ass up and land this thing."

Dingo pulled away from me. "I told you I made some changes," he said. "Push the red button and it will take us down."

I punched the red button. Fifteen minutes later, we landed at the Midland Airport. Dingo awoke enough to taxi to the hangar area. I decided that I would kill the alien after we were over this and he had cleared me of the murder charges. Dingo, though, got out of the plane and walked to a truck that seemingly was waiting for us. With each step, the alien awoke a bit more and showed no trace of hangover or drunkenness. Enochians metabolize alcohol different than we do, I reminded myself. I followed him to the truck.

"Come on, Captain," he said. "We don't have any time to waste."

"Yeah," I mumbled to myself, "I'm definitely going to kill him."

14

We stopped in front of a modest house on Gulf Avenue on the west side of Midland and double-checked the address. Dingo and I got out and walked to the door. I could hear a child's song playing from inside when I punched the door-bell. I sang along with the tune.

"And Dingo was his name-O," I sang and glanced at Dingo. The blue alien, standing out of the line of sight from the door, puffed his jowls at me. I smiled. "Serves you right for scaring the hell out of me in the plane." The door opened. A teenage girl greeted us. I spoke before she did.

"Good afternoon, ma'am," I said in my best polite southern drawl. "We're trying to get in touch with Denise Windham."

"She's not home right now, but . . ." She let her words trail off, as Dingo stepped into her view. "You're an Enochian, aren't you?"

Dingo matched my drawl as best he could. "Yes ma'am. Will Ms. Windham be back soon?"

"Oh, yeah," the girl said, her excitement evident. "And I would love to have you wait for her. I'm Kristen, her daughter."

Kristen opened the door wider and showed us to the living room. A younger girl, about four, sat mesmerized by a sing-along tape. When the song ended, the four-year-old reached up and punched the rewind button. The song started again. Dingo puffed his jowls, but said nothing. I figured that he would want to get hold of that dog named Bingo.

"May I offer you something to drink?" I swear she couldn't have been more than sixteen, but she had the manner of someone older. Dingo declined her offer and tried to ignore the music.

"Yes, please," I answered. "Water or tea, if you have it." The girl went to the kitchen to fix the drink. I couldn't help but wonder what her mother would say, since she invited two strangers into their house. I would be livid. *Maybe Midland is different from New Orleans,* I thought. I really doubted it was that different.

She came back with the drinks, and sat down in a chair facing the two of us on the couch. She spoke to Dingo. "When Mother was researching her book, I used to go with her to the Rejected Enochian Reservation all the time," she said, studying the alien closely. "I can't say that I remember you." The girl began clicking and whistling at the alien. Dingo looked surprised, but he answered her question. The girl nodded. "Yeah, that would explain it."

"Explain what?" I asked. She looked at me, quizzically. I shrugged. "I don't speak Enochian."

"Oh," she replied. "Mr. (she whistled and clicked) has been off the reservation for a very long time." She looked at Dingo and pouted. "I think he was rejected by the Rejected, though he denies it."

Dingo puffed as the child's song ended once more. "I do deny it," he said. "I left the reservation on my own accord, thank you."

The four-year-old was about to punch the rewind button again. The girl turned. "Freddie, turn that off and come and meet someone." Freddie turned around and walked to the teenager, then climbed in her lap. Freddie's lips pushed out and her eyes narrowed as she studied Dingo.

"Why you blue?" Freddie scrunched up her red eyebrows and played with her red hair as she asked the question.

"Freddie, this is (click and whistle)," the teenager said softly to the child. "He was born a long way away on a whole different planet, not on Earth."

The child seemed to consider what Kristen told her and then repeated her question. "But why you blue and what's your name?"

Dingo laughed. "I'm blue because that's just the way I'm made, Freddie. Just like you were made with red hair." Freddie nodded. "And you can call me Dingo. That's easier than my real name, isn't it?"

"Dingo?" Freddie questioned. The four-year-old pondered that briefly and started to sing. "D-I-N-G-O and Dingo was his name-O." To my surprise, Dingo smiled and laughed at the child's song.

Maybe there was hope for him. It won him a reprieve. I decided not to kill him.

Freddie turned to me, still giggling at the blue alien. "What's your name? I'm Freddie."

As I was about to answer, I heard a door open and a woman's voice call out. "Kristen, I'm home." Paper rustled in the hall. The door shut and I heard the jingle of keys followed by a grunt of effort.

"That's Mom," the teenager said to us. She got up to help with the groceries. Dingo and I stood also and faced the direction of the woman's voice.

"Kristen, whose truck is that parked out front?" I heard irritation in her voice, which was getting closer. "I told you that you couldn't have visitors when you were babysitting Freddie for the Jacksons." Windham came around the corner and stopped. She dropped the two bags she was holding, when she saw Dingo. Her mouth fell open.

"Mom, this is (click and whistle) or Dingo, as he is called in English," Kristen said, sporting a mischievous grin and twinkling eyes.

"He's funny and blue," Freddie said.

Windham shook her head as if to clear it. "I can see that, Freddie. Thank you." Windham reached down and picked up the two bags she had dropped and gave them to Kristen. "Young lady, we'll talk about you letting strangers into the house later." Kristen lost her smile, but didn't say anything. Windham glanced at us, but turned back to her daughter. "Get the rest of the groceries out of the van and put them up. Then, you take Freddie home to Trish while I find out what our visitors want."

Kristen smiled at Dingo and left, dragging the protesting Freddie by the hand. Windham turned to face us.

"Ms. Windham," I began. She held up a hand to stop me as she walked around the couch. Windham walked up to the tall alien. I guessed the blonde-haired woman was about five-eight, but she looked up into the alien's yellow eyes, then clicked and whistled at him. I recognized the tone from the experimental subjects of the past. She was challenging Dingo. Dingo took a step back and responded in kind. The two stared at each other. I didn't know what to expect next, but I knew that Dingo could take her; however, she had more guts than I did. I don't think I would have challenged a six-five, three-hundred-fifty-pound alien.

Windham clicked and whistled at Dingo again, and I saw the alien relax as he answered. Something important had just happened, and I wasn't sure what. The woman clicked again, but I interrupted with a wolf whistle of my own. Dingo puffed his jowls at me and Windham glared, first at me, then back at Dingo.

"Look," I said, "I don't speak Enochian and we don't

have time for games. Ms. Windham, we need your help."
Neither of them seemed to hear me. They continued to
glare at one another. "Ms. Windham, I know that this is
probably some type of wonderful Enochian custom that
you're acting out and displaying with Dingo, but time is an
important consideration."

"Unfortunately, my friend here is not trying to be rude,"
Dingo said. He puffed and sat down, so as not to be as in-
timidating. "And he also happens to be correct. Time is an
important consideration for our business." He looked up at
the woman. "We do need your help, Dr. Windham."

"Doctor?" There was no such appendage on her name in
her book.

Windham relaxed and favored me with a half-smile. She
looked as young as her daughter did. "Doctor of Anthropology," she said. "My doctoral dissertation formed the
major part of the book I wrote on the Enochian Rejected."
She sat in the chair opposite the couch. I sat beside Dingo
and watched her frown. "I suppose it's my book that
brought you here, though I don't know what I can do to
help you." She looked at Dingo. The glaring and seeming
animosity between them was gone.

Dingo cleared his throat, another of his human gestures.
"Dr. Windham, we need access to the Enochian Reservation."

"You should have access," Windham said. "All the Rejected have access to the reservation."

"It's not as simple as that," Dingo said stroking a jowl.
"You see, I'm *persona non grata* among the Rejected."

Windham nodded. This did not surprise her. However, I
was extremely interested, since Dingo had not discussed his
background, while knowing all about mine.

"Why aren't you welcome among your own people?"

They both turned to look at me.

Windham studied my face, obviously wondering where she had seen me before, but she did not ask. Instead, she answered my question. "Dingo has abandoned his people for the favor of humans," Windham said. She rubbed her eyes. "As a matter of fact, any Enochian who sees Dingo is supposed to kill him on sight." She turned to Dingo. "Isn't that right?"

Dingo puffed his jowls in response. I couldn't tell if it was a shrug or disgust. Windham knew, but she wasn't saying.

"If you get onto the reservation," I said to Dingo, "then you are not likely to get out, are you?"

"I'll get out with every bit of my blue skin," Dingo said forcibly. "Those fools could not stop me."

I saw Windham raise an eyebrow. "What is so important that you would risk your life and (clicks and whistles) to go to the reservation?" she said, and then turned to me. "The word would loosely translate as 'pride' in English, but it's much, much more than that."

"Much more than pride," Dingo agreed, nodding at me. "The term deals with the essential nature of Enochian life. Pride is a small part, but the rest is untranslatable into human language or human understanding, though your species does possess the trait." He turned back to Windham. "I am amazed, Doctor, of the breadth of your knowledge about our culture."

"You haven't answered my question," she said, and then she clicked at him.

Dingo laughed. I began to think that his laughter exposed a nervous tic, or that Enochians didn't really understand humor that well. *Come to think of it, I'm not sure humans understand humor that well either,* I thought.

105

Windham waited while the alien shivered with mirth. Dingo steadied himself and turned serious. His eyes betrayed anger and a fierceness I had not seen before, when he looked at Windham again.

"I must go to the reservation because someone is trying to kill the Prefect, which would precipitate a restart of the War," Dingo said. He was quiet for a few moments, letting the words sink in.

I knew that we were lucky the first time, and that we wouldn't be so lucky in a second encounter with the Enochians. Finding the mutated gene and the virus that affected only Enochians had been an accident, fortuitous perhaps, but still an accident. The Enochians had the antidote, though, and it was unlikely that they would hold back if a new war erupted. Of course, I knew that Earth leaders had been developing nasty surprises for the Enochians should they come back in force. I just wasn't privy to the new weapons.

"Your President Gamble is also in danger," Dingo continued, "but I believe the real target is the Prefect of the Enochian homeworld."

15

Windham was quiet for a few moments, digesting the information from Dingo. While she did, I looked at her. What I saw I liked. I judged her to be in her late thirties, early forties. Her shoulder-length blonde hair had a touch of whiteness coming on around her face. A slightly downturned mouth told me that she did not smile enough, but I figured she would be very pretty with a smile. I imagined her laughing, and then I caught myself.

I rubbed my eyes and wondered how tired I must be that I would begin fantasizing about a woman I'd met less than ten minutes ago. Looking away, I tried to hide my embarrassment. Having worked the night shift for the last five years, I didn't meet many new people, being on the wrong schedule for socializing. Most of the women I had met were doctors, nurses, or paramedics. Patients didn't count. People came to the emergency room because something was wrong. I couldn't take advantage of someone in a time of weakness. Still, it would be nice to talk with someone who didn't share my occupational cynicism about the world.

I glanced back at Windham and noticed that she was staring at me, as though still trying to figure out where she had seen my face. She didn't look away when I noticed. I squirmed a little on her couch, self-conscious of the scrutiny, especially since I had been scrutinizing her a few seconds before. I was sure she wasn't thinking nice things about me.

"Where do you fit into all this?"

She asked me a direct question, so I gave her a direct answer. "A drunk Enochian came into my emergency room and started shooting off his mouth about a conspiracy to kill the President."

She nodded, opening her mouth to speak, but I held up a hand to indicate I wasn't through.

"And since then," I said, "I have been shot at, had a grenade thrown into my apartment, set up for a murder rap, informed that all of my coworkers for that night had been murdered, ambushed in a morgue, got into a fight in a Louisiana rest stop with two rednecks, flown to Midland Texas by a drunk Enochian, and now I have to beg a woman who has never seen me before to smuggle me onto an alien reservation."

Windham raised her eyebrows at me, as I took a deep breath to continue.

"My life hasn't been this exciting since the War, so I do happen to believe that Dingo is telling the truth," I said, glancing at Dingo. I hedged on that last statement. "He may not be telling me the truth about everything, but on the assassination attempt, I don't think I can doubt him."

Windham sighed. "You're wanted for murder. Just wait till I have that talk with Kristen." Windham continued to scrutinize me. "You don't look like a murderer, but the news is not where I've seen your face. Somewhere else." Windham brushed hair from her face.

"To you, he does not look like a murderer," Dingo said. "But to many of my people, Captain Roger Stimson of the U.S. Army Intelligence Biological and Chemical Warfare Unit is a mass killer on a planet-wide scale." Dingo sounded proud of my status as Earth's most productive mass murderer, as if what I had done deserved a badge of honor rather than the guilt and shame I had been carrying for so long.

Windham raised both eyebrows at the alien and then

scrunched them up in thought. "The virus?" She looked at Dingo. He nodded. Windham turned to me. "You were the one who released the alien virus and ended the War." It was a statement. To me, it sounded like a judgment and conviction.

Windham wasn't looking at me anymore. I tried to put the pleasant fantasies about the woman out of my mind. My background in the War would kill any chance of a friendship with the anthropologist who had befriended the Rejected Enochians. The guilt of my actions fell heavy on my chest as I hung my head. I looked up as she spoke to me again.

"You're the one they court-martialed after the War," she said. I could have sworn there was excitement in her voice. "You let the virus loose without authorization, and the politicos tried to get you for war crimes."

"We were losing," I said, softly. "The politicians would have never made the decision, but I didn't release the virus without authorization. I just couldn't prove I had been given orders from my commanding officer."

Thinking of Boudreau made my anger rise, drowning out my guilt. General Boudreau gave me orders that implied that I should release the virus when it was ready. I remembered his outrage as Congress and others began attacking our use of a biological agent on the invaders. All of them, including Boudreau, conveniently forgot that, without the virus, we would have lost the War. Windham brought me back to the present.

"It wasn't necessary, but you didn't know that," Windham said, absently. "God, it must have killed millions of Enochians."

"Close to a billion," Dingo said. He sounded almost cheerful about the fact.

I sank deeper into the couch as they talked. "I am well aware of the disaster I unleashed upon the Enochians, but with the information I had then, I'd do it again." I sat up straight. "I'm not proud of what I did, but I did the right thing, militarily. The tribunal backed me up."

Windham looked concerned. "The guilt must be fantastic," she said, almost whispering. "I'm sorry."

I looked down and shrugged. "The guilt was a major factor in my becoming a nurse."

"Makes sense," Windham said. "You spend your life helping others as a penance for the guilt." She turned to Dingo. "He doesn't know, does he?" Windham addressed the question to Dingo. He must have shaken his head. I didn't look. "A formidable enemy, indeed. I'll get you guys onto the reservation."

I looked up. She smiled at me. I was wrong; she wasn't pretty when she smiled. She was beautiful. I felt old stirrings rise within me, feeling like a teenager again.

"I've got to see their reaction when Dingo introduces you," she said, laughing. "You might even let Dingo keep his life and pride." She stopped and thought for a moment. "If this assassination attempt is going to be in New Orleans in less than forty-eight hours, then how will going to the reservation help avoid it?"

She had a point. Up until now, I had been running from too many things and letting Dingo take me wherever he wanted to go. I had no idea as to the rhyme or reason for going to the Enochian Reservation. I just plain ran because I had nothing else to do. Dingo appeared to have a plan. I frowned.

"The Enochian who has been trying to kill both myself and the Captain came from the reservation." Dingo stopped and looked at both us, as if wondering how much information he should divulge. He gazed at me. "The fact that you are a formidable enemy would give you a place of honor at home, but I'm afraid that you might be in danger on the reservation, Captain." Dingo puffed. "There are those who think like your politicians at the end of the Human War, that you are not a 'formidable enemy,' but a criminal. They want Earth destroyed for what humanity did to Enochians."

"I don't understand," I said. "If that's the case, then why not just drop a dinosaur killer asteroid on us and be done with it?"

"The Prefect has decided that Earth has proven worthy of trade and friendship for those same actions, Captain," Dingo said. "We have Enochians who are plotting to kill the Prefect for the sole purpose of destroying your planet, in much the same way you almost destroyed ours." Dingo took a deep breath. "These Enochian traitors have formed an alliance with the Sons of Earth, though the Sons of Earth do not have the entire story, of course." Windham groaned at the mention of the Sons of Earth. Dingo ignored her. "An assassination and ultimate war between our species will morally be the end of the Enochian confederation. We would sink into turmoil. Not to mention the fact that Earth and humans would be utterly destroyed in the process." Dingo fell silent, a silence that affected all of us.

I didn't take exception to Dingo's relegating Earth's destruction to a response to a consequence. He was thinking like an Enochian, not like the humans he had been around for so long. His long assessment of the situation strengthened my resolve to see this through, even if I was being manipulated.

"When do we get started?" Windham said, breaking our silence.

"We must leave for the airport immediately," Dingo said. "I have contacts that can provide transportation to the reservation."

Windham looked the two of us over and sniffed loudly. "I've got some things I need to do, such as getting my daughter taken care of for the next couple of days. Why don't you two take the time to clean up? I feel sure it's a small plane."

Dingo puffed, but I thanked her. I needed a shower, just to feel human again. As for Dingo's Enochian smell, I had gotten used to it, but it was beginning to make my nose run after being with him for twenty-four hours. She grabbed a couple of towels, leading Dingo to one bathroom and me to another.

Windham studied what I was wearing, but left without saying anything. I stripped and got into the shower. Hot water ran down my back and I began to feel refreshed. I rinsed with cold water to wake me up. As I got out of the shower, I noticed that a pink bathrobe was hanging beside the towel. My filthy clothes were gone. I dried and put on the robe, pulling it as tight as I could, and walked into Windham's bedroom.

Toweling my hair a bit more, I noticed a picture of a young man on Windham's dresser. He was in uniform, smiling for the camera. A little girl sat on his knee with her arms around him. I assumed the girl to be Kristen, the daughter. I picked up the picture. He looked like many of the young, overly cocky officers who went out to face a superior technological force. Most of them died in the opening months of the War.

The picture brought memories of my wife to mind. Belinda had been visiting her parents in Los Angeles when the aliens attacked. The Enochians claimed that the destruction of L.A. had been an accident. Half a million people lost their lives in the attack, including Belinda. And I lost my innocence that day twelve years ago. I'd sworn I would get even with the aliens.

Guilt flooded my mind as I thought of the virus. There's only one thing I would never tell anyone about the decision to release a fatal virus among the aliens. That decision was made for revenge and revenge only. They took away my life, so I decided to take away as many of their lives as I possibly could.

That is why Bio-Chem was so efficient and effective, during the War. Every step we took was for one reason—to avenge Belinda's death. Guilt overwhelmed me as I thought of the carnage I created on the battlefield and on the Enochian homeworld. Tears streamed down my face as I remembered my reaction, and my emotions when I realized that killing the Enochians would not bring Belinda back. All I had succeeded in doing was creating a lot more sentient beings with the sense of grief and loss I had. It did not help me get over Belinda. Tears rolled down my face as I stood, holding a picture of a soldier I never knew.

"He was my husband." I jumped at the sound of Windham's voice. I turned to look at her with tear-filled eyes. "Mr. Stimson, are you all right?" The concern in her voice sounded genuine.

"Yes," I said wiping tears from my face and eyes. I controlled the flow of tears by shutting them off and banishing the memory of my long-dead wife. My grief over Belinda's death returned to the recesses of my mind, where I separated her from the actions I had taken in her name. Under control, I looked at the picture in my hand. "Did he die in the War?"

She nodded.

"I lost my wife at the War's onset," I said. "She was in Los Angeles during the initial attack. I guess I've never really gotten over it."

She walked in and put a hand on my shoulder.

"I'm fine, really. Fatigue and your husband's picture overtook my emotions." I looked around. "Where are my clothes?"

"Being washed, along with Dingo's garb," she said. "If I'm going to spend any length of time in a small plane with the two of you, then I'm not going to smell your odors, if I can help it."

I laughed.

She squeezed my shoulder. "Are you sure you're okay?"

"I'm fine," I said. "Nothing wrong with me that eight hours of sleep that I won't get couldn't cure."

She took her husband's picture from me and sat down on the bed. "I hated them when Richard was killed," she said, smiling sadly at the picture. She looked up. "Eight years ago, at the end of the War, I would have been real proud to have met you." She laughed a little. "As a matter-of-fact, I joined an organization that had formed to provide for your defense fund against the charges at your court-martial."

I remembered the defense fund had been established for me, but neither I, nor any of my lawyers, ever saw a dime of the money. It was then that the name James Williams became nationally known. "Did you know James Williams?"

She looked at me and made a face at my question. "I knew James," she said, shaking her head. "James started the fund in Dallas, which is where I was living at the time. James encouraged me to learn all I could about the Enochians. He always said, 'Got to know your enemies, Denise.' " She was quiet for a moment.

"Anyway, I entered the University of Texas in Arlington as a grad student in Anthropology. When it came time to write my thesis, I applied to the Enochian governing council for permission to study Enochian culture. No one expected approval from the Enochians or the United States government, least of all me, so I had not made any arrangements for the care of Kristen. When they accepted, they made special provisions for her in their school for their children. That's where she learned to speak the language. We stayed on the Enochian Reservation for over three years. I lost my hate of these people as I tried to understand them." She gazed at her husband's picture, grief and love evident in her look.

"If you study something and thoroughly understand it, if it is not inherently evil, you cannot hate anymore." Her eyes lost their focus as she stared at a closed window shade. Absently, she rubbed the picture of her husband and daughter. She took a deep breath and let it out slowly. Her eyes focused and she looked down at the picture.

"There is nothing inherently evil about the Enochians," Windham said, studying my face for a reaction. My emotions remained locked and under control, a trick I'd learned in the emergency room. "In their way, they are an honorable people. Probably more honorable than we are."

"How did you get linked with the Sons of Earth?" I wanted to know, because the Sons of Earth were involved in the actions that had sent me running from my home. But a bit of me did not want to think of the fact that I was alone with a woman I was attracted to in her bedroom, wearing nothing but one of her borrowed pink gowns. I was acutely aware of how attractive Windham was as she sat on the bed, pondering whether she would answer my question.

"James and I were engaged for a while," she said, wrinkling her nose as if she smelled something bad. "When I was approved for the study, James encouraged me to go, to learn everything I could about them. He didn't know that over the course of living with the aliens, I would change. Knowledge destroys hate and prejudice." She smiled.

"When the book was published, James leaked our relationship to the media. I was lucky to get this job at the University of Texas Permian Basin, much less being taken seriously by my peers."

Kristen walked into the room. "Mom, Dingo refuses to come out of my bathroom until he gets his clothes back."

I laughed at the thought of a modest alien. "Let me see what I can do." I went to the other bathroom and knocked. "Dingo, open up."

"Are you alone?"

I looked back at Windham and her daughter. Both of them smiled and went back into the living room.

"Just you and me," I told him through the door. "Now what seems to be the problem?"

"They took my clothes and left something that is not long enough," Dingo said, a pleading quality in his voice. I explained that Windham wanted to help us by washing our clothes.

"Besides," I said to the alien, "you were getting a bit gamey. And so was I." I heard him puff his jowls.

"Captain, I do not understand this obsession you humans have with smell. You don't appreciate the value of smell in knowing your enemies and your friends." Now his voice sounded petulant.

I smiled, sensing his discomfort. "Are you coming out or not?"

Dingo hesitated. "Captain, this thing is not long enough," he said, emphasizing the word "long."

I wondered what he was trying to tell me. A sudden flash of memory provided the answer. I remembered my examination of him in the emergency room. I made him strip to see if there were any other injuries and to check for any weapons he might have had hidden on his person, a precaution taught to me by an old nurse who'd mentored me when I first started. "A naked person can't shoot you, unless the gun is hidden in a body orifice," he had told me.

It was something I never forgot.

Anyway, the exam had shown that Dingo was quite male. I looked down at my own robe and laughed. If Dingo's robe was the same length, he was right. It would not have been long enough.

Windham stuck her head inside the bedroom and asked if there was anything she could do. I shrugged my shoulders and laughed harder. She looked at me, a question on her face, but finally she shrugged and left.

"Look, Dingo, tie the robe around your waist to cover up any appendages you do not want shown," I said, still laughing. "Besides, if you cover up, you won't be able to show off your tattoo."

Dingo puffed in disgust, but came out of the bathroom with the robed tied around him like a towel. "After this is over, we will never speak of this incident." The alien stood up straight and glared at me. The robe came untied and fell to the floor. Dingo looked surprised.

"Oh, my," Windham's voice said from the doorway. Dingo reached down, grabbed the robe, and bounded into the bathroom. He jumped too hard and I heard a crash. I collapsed on the floor and laughed, as Windham called out to him, "You'll pay for any damage you did, Enochian." She looked at me, sitting on the floor laughing, and started to giggle.

Dingo would not speak to us through the door and refused to come out of the bathroom until his clothes were returned to him. When the clothes were dry, he dressed and strode into the living room. Without stopping to look at us, he said, "We must leave, now."

Windham and I laughed all the way to the airport.

16

Windham and Dingo clicked and whistled at one another, while I watched the lights of west Texas and then New Mexico roll by underneath us. There had been no histrionics from me as we headed for take-off, but Dingo had not drunk the major part of three fifths of whiskey either. I sighed at the darkness and turned back to the plane cabin, which was lit with the glow of green light from the instrument panel.

I noticed Windham looking at me in the pale glow and I smiled. She looked pretty in the subdued lighting and I wanted to tell her so, but the fact that we were flying to an alien reservation on Earth, while I was wanted for murders that I did not commit, kept me from speaking my mind. That and the fact that less than two feet away from me was an Enochian whom I had just begun to think had somehow engineered this entire experience, especially my participation. Regardless of my suspicions about Dingo, I did not think he played a part in the murders of my friends.

Windham smiled back at me, and I thought she was going to say something, but she just sighed and glanced at Dingo. I looked back down at the darkness, wondering why I felt like a schoolboy whenever I looked at her. When I glanced back, Windham had closed her eyes, waiting for the plane ride to be over.

I sighed again and kept my eyes turned to the darkness below. It was just as well that she didn't speak. I was afraid I would let my boyish crush come too far to the surface. I felt foolish, a man almost forty feeling giddy about a woman I'd just met. It was time to think about other things, like how it was that Dingo seemed to be managing my life for the last couple of days.

The alien had already admitted that he came to my emergency room by design in an effort to solicit my help in his and the dead Enochian Bilbro's plan to foil an assassination attempt. And the fact that Dingo's story had changed since the emergency room visit rather bothered me. Why did he pick me? Was it my intelligence training? Or was it the fact that I was the instigator of a holocaust that made the German slaughter of the Jews in the middle of the last century look like a minor disagreement rather than the horror that it truly was? Dingo had said that I'd killed close to a billion individuals. I couldn't grasp that concept.

I glanced over at Dingo, who was leaning back in his seat, snoring, as the plane glided into the night. How much did I know about this creature? I had been following him blindly for the last twenty-four hours and over a thousand miles. He had connections with the Lanaka, which he had made clear over and over again. He was selling something of importance to the U.S. government or to private industry in return for the lavish lifestyle I had seen. I looked around the small plane. Something paid for this. And he had enough pull somewhere to have all of his communications and transportation devices altered to be invisible to human authorities. I wondered whether Dingo wasn't a member of the Lanaka, or maybe some other shadow agency of his government or my own.

This talk of assassination of the President and the Enochian Prefect may have been a plan to get me to the reservation to stand trial for my sins against the Enochian civilization. I shuddered at the thought, but the guilt I felt for my responsibility edged me toward accepting my fate, if that were the case. If Dingo were an Enochian agent of some sort, then I might not face a trial on Earth, but on Enoch itself.

I shook my head. I had begun to start fantasizing the outcomes of all this activity. There was no way that I was going to know what was going to happen. It felt to me that Dingo was the puppet master pulling my strings. I looked at the alien again, but perhaps he was as much puppet as I was. If that were the case, then the three of us could be in for a lot of trouble when we arrived at the reservation. An alarm chimed on the console in front of Dingo.

Dingo sat up and rubbed first his eyes and then his jowls. He grinned at me before checking the readouts to find our location. "Looks like we are over Mescalero, Captain," he said. "I've got to land this thing manually, since I've never flown into this airport in this plane. The computer pilot doesn't know the landscape." He looked at the sleeping woman between us. "Better wake Denise up, so we will be at our best when we land."

"I'm awake," Windham said, yawning. She looked at me and smiled. "I wish I could call Kristen to make sure she's all right."

"If Dingo doesn't mind, I have his phone in the backpack," I said, reaching for the backpack. Dingo assented. Windham talked to her daughter, who was staying at Freddie's parents' house, and hung up the phone satisfied that Kristen was safe.

"Thank you," she said, handing the phone back to me. I nodded and replaced the phone in the backpack Windham had lent us. I wanted to get the laptop out of the bag and check the news, but the alien spoke and I decided to wait.

"We'll be going down soon," Dingo said.

I groaned. "Couldn't you say that another way?" Dingo laughed. Windham reached over, patted my hand, and tried to console my fear of flying. I liked her touch, but instead of looking at her, I looked at Dingo and frowned. Dingo was studying the map on the monitor in front of him while talking to the tower for clearance to land. I wondered how much I could trust this Enochian.

Windham leaned over and put her lips to my ear. I could smell her in the close quarters of the plane. I felt her breath in my ear as she said, "Your doubts are showing, Roger. From what I can tell, Dingo is trustworthy."

I wanted to believe her. With my crush, I desperately wanted to believe her, but all I could do was nod and try to soften my frown. Dingo led me to her. *If I can't trust him,* I thought, *what makes me think I can trust her?* I looked at the lights of the airport as we began our descent.

17

Mescalero was colder than Midland, so the light jacket I wore did not do enough to keep out the north wind, which blew in from the Sacramento Mountains. We got out of the plane and walked toward the terminal. The small airport, which had not existed before the War, had been built as a direct result of Apache interaction with the Enochian Reservation. A voice interrupted our silent trudge across the tarmac.

"I sure am glad you blue-skinned bastards came around, so the white man would forget about the old drunken Indian stereotype."

I stopped and turned toward the voice, ready for another fight like the one just outside of Lake Charles. I noticed the badge the Native American who had spoken wore on the outside of his jacket, which also carried an emblem identifying the Mescalero Sheriff's Office. *Is he here for me?* I wondered.

Dingo stopped and drew himself up to his full height, his head tilted slightly back. The Enochian sniffed loudly. "Captain," Dingo said without looking at me, "do you smell that incredibly awful smell? I think I smell a damned Apache."

For a few eternal seconds, no one said anything. I studied the other man, watching for his reaction. He wore a cowboy-type hat with no emblem, which covered dark brown, almost-black hair that spilled out from under the hat and down the back of his jacket. The man's face was rugged and windblown, with two dark, piercing eyes that reminded me of Devereaux. A rather large, crooked nose gave the impression that the man's face was lopsided. He looked older than I looked, but I guessed he wasn't that much older. The silence deepened and I began making preparations for my legal defense. The police officer and Dingo laughed at the same time, breaking the tension.

"Dingo, you blue son of a bitch, it's been too damn long since you've been here," the man said as he walked up to the alien and put a bear hug on him. He turned to look at Windham and me. "Dr. Windham," he said, slightly bowing to her. "I am honored to make your acquaintance."

"Why, thank you," Windham said, blushing, "but how—"

He held up a hand. "I read your book, Doctor, and I was impressed by your insight into the Enochian culture." He looked thoughtful. "Perhaps you could do a study on the Mescalero Apaches one day. I think the council would approve of you."

"Well, I really haven't done the field work or the theoretical studies for a Native American culture," Windham said, still blushing ever so slightly. The color animated her face, even in the muted light outside the terminal. "Who are you?" she asked in a nice way. The officer looked at Dingo, who clicked and whistled at him. Windham said, "That's all right. Just do it, now."

"I'm sorry," Dingo began. "I do forget the human niceties, sometimes." He puffed his jowls. "Anyway, this is Joe Martinez, the sheriff for the Mescalero Apache Reservation." Dingo did not introduce us, which led me to believe that Martinez already knew who I was.

"Pleased to meet you," he said, bowing slightly toward Windham. I saw her blush come back. I was not happy with the attention given to her by the sheriff. Martinez glanced at me and gave me the barest of nods before returning his attention to Windham. I tried not to let my jealousy and uneasiness show. I don't think I succeeded.

"Dr. Windham, I really meant that about you doing a study on the Apaches," Martinez said and then smiled suddenly. "Perhaps you could study the effects of the increased trade between the reservation and the Enochians just to our west."

Windham wrinkled her brow, thinking. "That would probably be interesting, hmm. I'll give it some thought, but right now, I've got my sights set on that building about fifty feet in front of me. It looks a lot warmer than I feel."

"No, you are coming with me," Martinez said to her. He turned to Dingo. "If I don't take you home, Cassandra will have my hide. She's cooked a special meal for you, Dingo."

The thought of food, a hot meal after all the running on this day, overcame my apprehensions. If Martinez was going to arrest me, then at least I was going to go to jail on a full stomach. I also felt better knowing that he had a wife. He led us to his truck. Dingo and the sheriff got into the front, while I shared the back with Windham. Dingo and Martinez caught up on the past.

"Damn, Joe, the place sure has changed in the last three years," Dingo said, as we rode through the downtown area of Mescalero. "It looks like there are about ten thousand people here now."

"Closer to fifteen thousand," Martinez said, nodding at Dingo.

The alien turned around in the seat carefully to speak to me. "Captain, you may not believe it, but the little metropolis we are riding through only had about a thousand people in it before the War."

"Yeah," Martinez agreed, "when I was first elected sheriff, just after the War, about eight years ago, the only people here were Apache, but with the Enochian trade that only goes through our town, we have just boomed." Martinez hesitated, calculating, then nodded. "That trade started just after your book came out, Dr. Windham. It became required reading for everyone here."

"Do you have much contact with the Enochians?" Windham asked.

Martinez scratched under the back of his hat before answering. "Not as much as we did just last week," he said. "Dingo, after dinner, we need to discuss your situation and his." Martinez jerked his thumb toward me. "There is something going on over there with the Enochians. It may not be safe."

Martinez turned into a driveway at the edge of the main town area. "I don't know for a fact. I've just got a feeling."

He was quiet as he stopped the truck, killed the ignition, and turned off the lights. He turned toward Dingo. "But like I said, we'll talk after dinner."

Martinez's wife was a beautiful woman. Because of her and the fact that she only looked to be in her mid-to-late twenties, I brought his age closer to mine. He might have been younger, but I doubted it. Cassandra Martinez welcomed us into her house with open arms and much commotion over the arrival of Dingo.

"Cassie," the alien exclaimed, sweeping the short, Native American woman up into his arms, planting an Enochian kiss on her cheek, "I have surely missed you. Not him, but you."

"Put me down, you idiot," she said, smiling at Dingo. I noticed Windham watching in fascination at Dingo's interaction with the Martinezes. Cassandra Martinez sniffed the air around her and then put her nose up to Dingo's chest. "Someone made you bathe, thank God."

Dingo stroked a jowl. "Yes, humans do not appreciate the wonderful Enochian smell. Not like you do, eh, Cassie?"

Windham's eyes momentarily widened, but she masked

her surprise at the sexual innuendo between an Enochian and a human as quickly as she had shown it.

Hell, I was shocked. I had never heard of any sexual interaction between the two species. I knew that Enochians and humans could not produce children, but I guess I had never considered the possibility of sexual union. I thought further on the subject and realized I had never heard anything about Enochian sexual unions at all. The aliens were very secretive about such things.

Mrs. Martinez slapped Dingo on the chest and turned to her husband. "Joe, you can shoot him anytime you like."

Martinez shrugged. "If he can stand you, then it's okay with me."

Mrs. Martinez took a towel off the apron she was wearing and launched it toward her husband's face. He caught it and nodded. "All right, I'll kill him later for the insult to you, but can we eat first? I think these people are starving."

Mrs. Martinez looked us over and extended a hand toward Windham. "Dr. Windham, it is an honor to have you dining with us."

Windham took the younger woman's hand and squeezed gently. "No, Mrs. Martinez, I am honored and grateful for your hospitality, especially at such short notice. And call me Denise, please." Denise smiled at her.

"Then you call me Cassie," she said, pleased with Windham's attention and graciousness. "Everyone around here does."

"And this gentleman to my right," Denise continued, "is Roger Stimson."

"Just Roger, please ma'am," I said, drawling. "I would like to thank you and your husband for your hospitality, also."

The woman smiled. "Any friend of Dingo's that brings him back this way will always be welcomed in this house."

She led us into the dining room. "Please be seated, and I'll be with you in a minute." She turned to her husband, who had followed us with Dingo into the dining room.

"Joe, go say goodnight to Maria and tell her to go to sleep, please," she said. "She threw a fit when you left, so go settle her down before she comes bursting out here—" Mrs. Martinez did not get a chance to finish.

"Daddy," yelled a two-year-old little girl as she ran through the living room toward her father. Martinez scooped her up while she was in full gallop and swung her up onto his shoulder, fireman style.

Maria squealed.

"A child," Dingo said, sounding awed and respectfully delighted. "Joe, you didn't tell me."

"That's what happens when you stay gone so long," the sheriff said. "Besides, I didn't want to spring you on her until I got a chance to warn her about big, bad, ugly aliens."

Maria rose up and looked at her father and then at Dingo. "Ugly aliens," she said, seriously. Martinez and Dingo laughed. Dingo cooed at her and the little girl cooed back, as Martinez took her toward the bedroom to put her back into bed.

"She takes after you, Cassie," Dingo said. "And she sure is lucky, 'cause she could have looked like Joe."

Cassandra ignored Dingo's insult of her husband. "Sit down, you old fool," she said, smiling. "Let me get the food."

"Do you need any help?" I asked.

"No," she said, shaking her head. "You are our guests. Stay seated and enjoy."

Martinez came out of the bedroom and went directly into the kitchen to help his wife with the food. With everything served, Dingo on my left grabbed my hand and nodded at me to bow my head. Denise grabbed my right hand and we bowed.

"We do not pray aloud because I am Catholic and Cassie will not accept anything but the tribal customs," Martinez said to us. "So we show a moment of silent respect for the gifts in front of us, each in our own way."

I said my thanks for the food, but could not find anything else for which to be thankful. I was still wanted for murder, as well as having someone out there trying to kill me. Both Enochians and humans had shot at me in the last couple of days. I tried to keep my feelings below my exterior. Dingo released my hand and began eagerly grabbing for plates of roast beef and mashed potatoes. Martinez spoke to me for the first time.

"So, Captain Stimson," Martinez said, as he ladled gravy over the potatoes and meat. "You're from New Orleans, I hear." He looked up at me and stared hard. After a moment, he yelped in pain and put down the gravy bowl. Turning to his wife, he asked, "Why did you kick me?"

She looked him square in the eyes. "You will not conduct your business at my dinner table." He looked incredulous for a moment and then yelled again as I heard her shoe hit shinbone. "Period!" Cassandra stared at her husband. He broke eye contact first.

I could hear the bruises growing on his leg. Martinez leaned down and rubbed his leg for a minute as his wife turned to Denise, smiled, and asked about her child, Kristen. We ate the rest of dinner with small talk. I did talk about New Orleans, inviting all of them to a Mardi Gras in the future, sometime when my apartment wasn't full of holes, but in keeping with Cassie's rules, I didn't mention my unique problems. It was after dinner before we talked business, the sheriff and I.

18

Mrs. Martinez began clearing the plates off the table, when it became obvious that everyone had eaten everything that they could eat. Dingo had eaten the most, but was careful to let others eat their fill before demolishing the rest of the meat and potatoes. Dingo offered to help clean the table, and Mrs. Martinez accepted. Denise got up to help, also.

"I'll wash, you dry," Dingo said to Denise. The three of them left the dining room with the dishes. Martinez motioned for me to follow him into the living room.

"Have a seat, Captain Stimson," he said, pointing at a chair across from the couch upon which he plopped.

"I'm not a captain anymore," I said as I sat on the edge of the chair, leaning slightly toward the Apache sheriff. "Dingo insists upon calling me that."

"You were in the Army, though." I nodded toward him in agreement. He lit a pipe and took a long drag, holding it in his lungs for a second before letting the smoke escape through his slightly opened mouth and his nose. "You are the Roger Stimson who was court-martialed after the War, right?"

I took a deep breath before answering. "Yeah, that's me. I was acquitted of any wrongdoing."

"I know," he said, nodding. "We were all pulling for you. The damn government was looking for a scapegoat for their conscience. Some congressmen called you the new Hitler. They said that releasing the virus was a genocidal act, a war crime." He took another long puff on the pipe.

"Hell, I fought in the damn War, unlike those politicians. We were just glad the damn thing was over." He was quiet, his eyes on some battlefield from a distant past. I understood the solitude in his memories.

"The politicians said we could have won without the virus," he said. "But every person I fought with knew we were losing." He smiled as he heard Dingo in the kitchen, bantering with the two women. "But that's ancient history as far as Mescalero is concerned. We've made our peace with the Enochians. As a matter of fact, we have done quite well."

After another long draw of the pipe, Martinez sat up and looked at me hard. His dark brown eyes measured me in a much deeper way than Devereaux had, as if he were peeling away my personality one layer at a time. "But that distant past still haunts you, doesn't it, Stimson?"

I hesitated before answering. "Yeah, in a way."

"You feel like you should have been convicted of genocide?" Martinez studied my reactions.

I shrugged, but didn't answer, while staring hard into his eyes. He already knew the answer to his question.

"You are also wanted for murder in New Orleans," he said, evenly. I nodded and tried not to show my uneasiness. "Wondering why I haven't arrested you?"

I shrugged again. "Sheriff, I assumed that Dingo had talked to you. He's my alibi for Devereaux's murder."

Martinez laughed. "Dingo's one hell of an alibi," he said, still chuckling. "The Feds are looking for him. I've even had some inquiries from the Enochians about his whereabouts. And they were not Enochians from the reservation, though they tried to pretend to be."

"How do you know?" I leaned forward. *Not from the reservation* meant that they had come from offworld. *How many Lanaka agents are on Earth?*

"I've dealt with the Enochians for the last eight years, since the end of the War," he said confidently. "I have my sources on the reservation."

He looked thoughtful, as if deciding what he should tell me next. He tried to take a drag on the pipe, but the fire had gone out. Muttering, Martinez reached for a cigarette in his front shirt pocket. For the third time that day, I wanted a cigarette.

"Sheriff, why haven't you arrested me and Dingo? Wouldn't your job be in jeopardy if you don't?"

He shook his head. "Hell, it's more likely my job would be gone if I did arrest Dingo." He laughed. "Dingo is the reason we were able to become the distribution point for the Enochian Reservation exports." He sat and thought for a moment, smiling.

"The first time I ever saw Dingo, I had arrested him for being drunk on the sidewalk at three in the morning. It was ten below that night and the fool didn't have a stitch of clothes on his ugly, blue body. Anyway, he didn't give me any trouble and, when he woke up the next morning, he said he had a proposition for the town council. He set up the distribution plan, which is why we are the only distribution point for the Enochians.

"He said he was thrown off the reservation for that specific purpose, to make the Enochians a wealthy people on Earth." Martinez took a drag of his cigarette and tapped the ash into the ashtray beside the couch. "But just like those Enochians checking on our friend in the kitchen, Dingo has never lived on the reservation." He paused, letting the information sink into my brain. "Dingo is not one of the Rejected."

If that were true, then Dingo could have ulterior motives besides the protection of the Enochian Prefect and the American

President. I leaned back in the chair and stared over Martinez's head, lost in my thoughts. I remembered the night he had come into the emergency room. He wasn't hurt that badly and could have certainly walked away from the incident. Two fifths of whiskey is not that much of a challenge for the liver of a three-hundred-fifty-pound alien. *No, he definitely came to the ER to get me involved in his schemes.* My anger grew as I thought of Larry, Dr. Richards, and Shirley. Devereaux and that phony Secret Service agent were also victims of Dingo's scheme, whatever it was.

"Are you sure Dingo's not of the reservation?" Anger seeped, unwelcome, into my voice. Martinez nodded. "You're leaving too much out, Sheriff. How do you know?"

Martinez stumped out the cigarette in the ashtray beside him. "He doesn't appear anywhere in their records. Dingo does not exist, according to the Rejected."

"That's because I erased all of my personal records."

I jumped at the sound of Dingo's voice. He stood in the kitchen doorway, wiping his hands with a towel. Putting the towel on the door handle, he walked into the living room to join us. Martinez smiled as he lit another cigarette. My anger formed a knot in my stomach. I glared at Dingo. Denise, looking a bit concerned, and Mrs. Martinez followed the alien. The sheriff's wife broke an awkward silence.

"I'm going to check on Maria," she said to her husband. Martinez nodded at his wife and then studied Dingo and myself. I realized the sheriff was using the tactic of pitting allies against one another, which he had perfected in his law enforcement experience, but the tactic did not work unless one of the partners had doubts about the other. I had my doubts about Dingo.

"How did you wipe your records, if you can't hack into human computers?"

Martinez raised an eyebrow at my question.

Dingo puffed his jowls in disgust. "I have trouble understanding human logic, a contradiction in terms, I must say, and the other ways they think," Dingo said, shrugging. "As you may have noticed, I am not human. But Enochians I know like the back of my hand, which is about as Enochian as you can get," he said, holding the back of his hand in front of him. "I know Enochian logic, Captain."

"Stop with that 'Captain' shit," I said, as my anger exploded. "You've been using my past and my guilt associated with it to manipulate me all along. No more."

I stood up to face the much bigger alien, bringing my eyes to as close to level with his as I could. His bath had worn off, but I ignored his stink. "Enough is enough, Dingo. I want the whole, damn truth, or I'm turning myself in to the sheriff here and taking my chances with a jury in New Orleans."

Dingo's eyes never wavered. I could hear him clicking and whistling under his breath. I assumed my heritage was being questioned in a tongue that I would never learn, but I did not care. I wanted answers, even if I had to beat them out of the much bigger alien. He took a deep breath and puffed at me. His breath made me want to gag. He looked around and sat beside Martinez on the couch. I stood over him.

"This is not getting us anywhere," he started. Dingo turned to Martinez. "When did you check into my history, Joe?"

"When those offworld Enochians came asking me questions," the sheriff responded. "You could tell they had not had much contact with humans. I didn't know what kind of trouble you were in, which made me realize that I didn't know that much about your history." Martinez took a drag off the cigarette. "They had no record of you, and no one I had talked to could confirm that you existed at all."

"That's not unusual for Enochians, Sheriff," Denise said. "When an Enochian is rejected, then the culture itself will wipe him out of their collective memory. A Rejected Enochian is truly 'a man without a country,' no matter what he may later do that would help the society overall." Denise sat in the chair beside where I had been sitting. "Once an Enochian is Rejected, they can never be taken back into that society."

Dingo nodded at her. "That's true, Doctor, but the Prefect does have the right to reinstate some members, at the discretion of the Prefect."

Denise raised her eyebrows and opened her mouth to speak to Dingo, but closed it and looked up at me. "Are you going to stand there glaring all night?"

My glare turned to her. "I've had eight friends and colleagues killed over this thing's manipulations, and I'm charged with the murder of a New Orleans police detective, a murder that I did not commit, I might add. Dingo isn't even mentioned in the news reports at all. I want the damn truth."

My body stood erect, taut with anger and some fear. I knew that Dingo was stronger than me, but I was perfectly willing to fight. My hands pumped into fists and released numerous times before I realized what I was doing.

Denise didn't blink at my outburst. She reached up and grabbed one of my hands, and unclenched the fist. "Roger," she said, softly, "sit down and relax." She pulled me toward her. "When Dingo backed down from your challenge, it meant that he was going to give you his answers. If he had not sat down, then the sheriff's house would be a shambles by now and someone, probably you, would have been hurt."

Don't be so sure that I'd be the one hurt, I thought. I took a deep breath and tried to calm my anger.

"She's right, Stimson." I turned to look at Dingo. "You have the right to know what I know. I was going to tell you before we went onto the reservation anyway, because you do have the right to back out." Dingo puffed, glancing up at me and then to Denise. "This is going to be dangerous. You two are my backup plans." Denise pulled at my hand and I sat back down. My anger had exhausted me. Dingo removed an envelope from his pocket, puffed once, took a deep breath.

"Joe, in this envelope is a deathbed statement concerning my friend's innocence of all the charges pending against him," Dingo said, handing the letter to Martinez. "In that letter, it explains what happened at the Riverwalk and in the morgue. Stimson did not murder anyone. Although, he did kill one of the people who ambushed us in the morgue, but that was self-defense." The alien turned to me.

"Captain, I have never meant to leave you on the hook for any of these murders in an effort to gain your cooperation," Dingo said. I was unused to the seriousness of his voice and the directness of his explanations. "And, as for using your guilt over the development and release of the virus against my species, that is not why I picked you."

I said nothing, but looked from Windham to Dingo. My anger had ebbed somewhat, though the doubts remained.

"Roger, he picked you because you are the most visible warrior from our society," Denise said. "You ended the War against the Enochians, so I suspect that your fame is greater than any other alien that the Enochians have ever faced."

I was confused. "Why?" My guilt over the virus release

had dominated my life almost as long as the grief for my dead wife. I knew that both needed to end, but I did not know how to stop the emotions. "Why am I so important?"

"Because no one ever hurt them as much as you did," Denise said. "The Enochians have a concept that the most formidable friend and ally you can ever have is the foe that hurts you the most. In my studies of the Reject society, I had access to historical records of the eleven other conquests or wars that the Enochians have engaged in during the last fifteen centuries."

She piqued my interest. I'd never learned anything about Enochian history beyond what I needed to know to complete my mission. After the War, I tried to forget about the aliens.

Denise continued. "No other culture had ever fought them as fiercely or hurt them as much as we did. And they know that your decision, made without the support or approval of your superiors, was made in what you believed was the best interest of your race. On the Enochian homeworld, you would be hailed a hero, not a villain."

"That may not be exactly true, at this moment," Dingo said. "For the same reasons that you are revered on my homeworld, you are also greatly hated. Dr. Windham is right when she said that the fact that you hurt us in ways others could not, nor had not in the past, makes you a hero to most Enochians. We also realize that you gave out the antidote just as quickly, again without authorization, as you released the virus." Dingo puffed twice before continuing.

"But the fact that you almost single-handedly destroyed the Enochian Empire has brought an emotion that we learned from you in the past war between our peoples. You taught us revenge in your attacks against nonmilitary positions. You taught us to hate with your suicide bombers and your guerrilla warfare tactics. We had never encountered creatures that would decide to fight to the end, even in the face of an obviously technologically-superior race. To win the War to where you accepted our terms for your surrender, we began to suspect that we would have to destroy your planet. We did not realize that destruction is what you had planned for us."

Denise broke in with a question. "You mean that there are Enochians who are willing to throw out fifteen centuries' worth of ideas and traditions?" She was incredulous.

Dingo puffed. "Our culture was affected more by you than you were by us," he said, sadness tingeing his words. "For the first time in our recorded history, we found that our species could be mortal, that we could lose in warfare, and that we could be defeated. Because of you, Captain, there is a struggle for the future of the Enochian soul. I don't know if we will survive as a race that I will recognize." Dingo hung his head.

I took a deep breath and closed my eyes. Dingo had alluded to this situation at Denise's house in Midland, but now he gave us the background. No one said anything for a few minutes, until Martinez broke the uneasy silence.

"Dingo, I'm afraid that the division amongst Enochians is beginning to come to a head on the reservation."

Dingo looked up. "In what way, Joe?"

Martinez took a long drag on his cigarette before answering. "Nothing I can put my finger on, but my relations with the Enochian security chief Gintomen have been rather strained and formal for the last couple of weeks. Almost like he doesn't trust me. Gintomen and I have been working together for the last five years. It had been a close relationship." Martinez looked thoughtful.

"We have a problem with teenagers and tourists trying to

illegally gain access to the Enochian Reservation. Gintomen told me to make sure that humans stay off Enochian land. He said he could not be responsible for their safety."

Dingo rubbed his left jowl. "Is that all he said?"

Martinez smoked for a moment and puffed rings into the air. "He said that he was afraid for the safety of his family and mine." The sheriff shrugged. "Since then, we've talked only once, and I got the feeling that he was afraid that someone would hear him talking to me."

Martinez continued. "All of the human truckers that used to pick up from the Enochian warehouses were let go about the time of our last conversation," he said. "Only Enochians are delivering products and picking up supplies. And I've seen very few Enochians in the last week."

"They're sealing off the reservation." We turned toward Denise. "If Enochians have an internal problem, then they are going to solve it without the prying eyes of human society."

I noticed Dingo nodding, a faraway look in his eyes. I must have had a confused look on my face, because Denise sighed.

"After the War ended," she said, "no one heard anything about the Enochians for at least two years. Not even the ones on the reservation. Then, all of a sudden, Enochian technology started hitting the markets." She turned to Dingo. "That would have been about the time you showed up here in Mescalero. Anyway, it took the Enochians two years to reach a sort of consensus on what to do next."

"None of that was in your book," I said. My words had the tone of accusation.

"Because she's speculating," Dingo said. I thought I heard admiration in his voice. "And doing a damn good job of it, I might add. Continue, Dr. Windham, I'm fascinated."

Denise clicked and whistled at him and smiled. Dingo

laughed, but answered in English. "Yes, knowledge is a way to power. An old Enochian proverb."

"The only reason the Enochians would be closing themselves off to the outside world is to meet a threat, either internal or external," Denise continued. "I suspect that it is a little bit of both, considering the story you and Dingo have told me, Roger."

"The Sons of Earth?" I asked.

"And the Lanaka," Denise responded.

"The Lanaka?" I was confused again. Martinez raised an eyebrow. Dingo was stoic, rubbing a jowl. "But the dead Enochian in the New Orleans morgue—"

Denise interrupted my question with a question of her own to Dingo. "Did that Enochian, Bilbro, say that he was from the Lanaka?"

Dingo hesitated. "No, I think I made an assumption."

Denise nodded. "As a fellow anthropologist, and the resident Enochian expert on humans, don't you work directly for the Prefect?"

Dingo sat back on the couch and stroked a jowl. He didn't answer.

"Anthropologist?" I asked. "You mean to tell me that he's a scientist?"

Denise was making leaps of knowledge that I couldn't fathom. She ignored me and concentrated on Dingo. Her stare was as hostile as it had been in her house earlier in the day. Martinez raised an eyebrow, but said nothing. Denise clicked and whistled at Dingo. It sounded like a demand.

Dingo puffed once. "Yes, I work for the Prefect." He turned to Joe and me. "But I am not a spy. I'm more like a trade ambassador."

"Knowledge *is* power," Denise said, softly, and then turned to Martinez and myself. "Dingo is not a spy, but he does gather intelligence. Trade intelligence. His job is to find out what we have to offer the Enochians in the way of trade. I think his friend Bilbro was a part of the Enochian Prefect's honor guard."

Dingo did not deny it.

"The Enochians never wanted to destroy us," Denise said. "We essentially did the same thing to the Japanese in the nineteenth century. We showed up with a huge battleship and superior weapons and told the Japanese that they were opening their society to us, or else. The Enochians treated us the same way. All they wanted to do was open us up to trade on the most positive terms to them, by defeating us in battle. But all that changed when we defeated them."

"We had never known defeat," Dingo said. "And the virus could have destroyed our civilization. There are many Enochians who do not want trade with humans. They want to wipe the human species out, entirely." Dingo puffed. "I'm afraid for both of our species, Captain."

I knew that the Enochians could destroy Earth from space. Hell, like in all those science fiction books about aliens conquering our planet that the Enochians made obsolete, I knew that they could throw that dinosaur killer asteroid at us and that would be that—game over.

Dingo was studying me closely. But humanity had not thrown everything we had at the aliens either. He knew, or at least suspected, there was another virus that could be more deadly to Enochians than the one I had unleashed upon them. I nodded toward Dingo, but I wasn't ready to acknowledge that possibility yet. Besides, Dingo still had not told the whole truth.

"So far, I have driven and flown about a thousand miles with you," I said to Dingo. "This trip started with your planned appearance in my emergency room three nights ago. After the shoot-out in the morgue, I followed you because I really had no place to go. People were shooting at me, and the police wanted me for murder. But now," I nodded toward the letter lying on the coffee table beside the sheriff, "I believe that you are giving me ammunition to fight any criminal charges. Why should I follow you into a situation that will be dangerous at best? At worst, from the things that the sheriff has said, it could be suicidal."

Dingo didn't say anything.

I wanted to scream and lose my temper, but for some reason, I was calm. "Are the President and the Prefect in danger in New Orleans?"

"I did not make that up, Captain," Dingo said, a bit defensively. "But that is not the only danger here. I have to know what is happening on the reservation."

"Why?" I asked.

Denise cleared her throat and appeared to be about to answer, but the ringing phone interrupted her.

"Excuse me," Martinez said and stubbed out a cigarette as he got up to answer the phone.

I looked at Denise, but Dingo answered first. "Whatever is going to happen Monday in New Orleans was planned on the reservation," Dingo said. "If I can get to the right people, then I can disarm their entire plan." Dingo hesitated. "At least, that was what Bilbro was going to do." He turned to Denise. "I'm sorry, Dr. Windham, that I was not truthful with you before. Bilbro is a member of the Prefect's Honor Guard. Or I should say was."

"And since he has been killed, you are bound to finish his mission," she said. The Enochian puffed at her. "Dingo, I will help you in any way that I can."

They turned, as I knew they would, to me.

I took a deep breath and sighed. "Shit," I said to no one

in particular. "I'd be a dolt to believe you now."

"I can assure you, Roger," Denise said, putting a hand on mine, "Dingo is telling the complete truth this time. And he needs our help to finish this job. A job I believe you were trained for during the War."

I looked down at her hand. Her touch felt good and could have changed my mind, except for the fact that I had already decided to go with Dingo. "You didn't let me finish," I told her. I gave her hand a squeeze and turned my attention to Dingo. "As I was saying, I'd have to be an idiot to believe that now you are telling the whole truth, but I have never been real smart."

Dingo sat up straight on the couch. "Thank you Captain, Denise."

I shrugged and asked, "When do we start?"

I was startled by a voice from the dining room. "You guys can ride out with me right now, if you wish," the sheriff said quietly. His voice had a sad quality to it. "Dingo, I don't know what's going on with those damn Enochian cousins of yours, but it has turned violent." Martinez hesitated as he lit another cigarette. "Three Apache teenagers went onto Enochian land early this afternoon. That was Gintomen on the phone. They have been murdered by an Enochian, it appears."

PART THREE

THE
RESERVATION

PROLOG

Excerpt from
Home of the Rejected: A Study of Enochians Abandoned,
by Denise Windham.

The Rejected Enochians live their lives as if they were on the homeworld of Enoch. Though they understand and accept that they are outcasts on Earth, left behind by a rapidly dying and retreating military force, the Rejected understand why they have been spurned by the rest of Enochian society. For one reason or another, each of the twelve thousand aliens left behind had been deemed as corrupted. Humans do not understand what corrupted them, and the Enochians themselves are not saying.

An essential part of being a rejected Enochian is making the most of one's position. These aliens understand that they can trade information and technology with the governments and peoples of Earth to better their own living conditions. For the most part, the United States and the rest of the world have accepted their entrepreneurial spirit and taken advantage of the influx of higher technologies in the world of electronics.

The one area that Enochians will not export to another species is information about their culture, their homeworld, and their dealings with each other within their own community. They are a very private species

145

with an innate sense of pride, for lack of a better term. Politeness marks their dealings with one another and the outside world. Though the culture of the Rejected is not without tension, that tension between their own will remain private and will not spill over into their dealings with humans. "Don't air your dirty laundry in public" is a concept that translates well to the Enochian mind.

19

We didn't leave immediately after the call about the murders. Sheriff Martinez spent some time on the phone out of our earshot, making some type of preparations. I thought it had to do with the autopsy for the three teens, but Denise just shook her head and looked concerned.

She was worried that the murders—the first of their kind anywhere near the Enochian Reservation—could be the first sign of a deteriorating situation on the reservation. If that were the case, then if I were Martinez, I would be preparing my people for the possibility of an armed excursion onto my land from the Enochians.

With the sheriff in the kitchen and Denise not talking, Dingo decided that I needed a little training in the art of fighting an unarmed Enochian. "If you challenge an Enochian like you did with me earlier tonight, then you had better be ready to fight," Dingo said with a serious tone I was not used to hearing. "An Enochian warrior, male or female, will not back down as I did earlier. On your feet, Captain."

I got up and faced him. "Dingo, I don't think we really have time for this."

Dingo listened for Martinez's voice in the kitchen. "We have time, Captain."

"And it is essential that you listen to him, Roger," Denise said. I turned to face her. "A challenge to an Enochian is not a habit you want to continue, unless you are prepared. Most times, it is a fight to the death. The only reason Dingo did not accept your challenge is that he understands humans."

"Denise, Dingo, I know what the challenges are," I said simply. "I was challenged a hundred times a day during the War."

"But do you know the weak points of the Enochian body?" Dingo asked.

My left leg flashed out from my body, with my foot stopping inches from an area just below the rib cage on the right side of Dingo's body. The alien flinched. I retracted my foot toward the ground. I kicked out my right leg and barely caught the alien behind the left knee. Dingo tumbled toward me. I backed up as he hit the ground and then jumped on top of him, facing his feet, and laid back hard with an elbow one inch away from what would have been the second cervical spine on a human. That area is a mound of flesh and nerve endings on an Enochian. A hard enough blow could have killed Dingo. As it was, I did not touch the mound.

I rolled off Dingo and hit the ground on all fours. I jumped to my feet as Dingo jumped to his. I saw the anger on his face. Rage burned just below the surface, and I wondered if maybe I should have hit him. I took a step back and held up both palms toward him. Dingo took a step toward me. I heard a high-pitched, shrill whistle and fierce clicking coming from Denise.

Dingo stopped and looked at her and then back to me. He puffed twice and tried to regain control. After a couple of seconds, I could see him physically relax his body. He did not offer to teach me any more about Enochian pressure points. "You're on your own, Captain," was all Dingo said.

"Dingo, I'm sorry if I hurt your pride," I said slowly, in

measured tones, so that he would know that I meant the apology. "But I was around Enochians for most of the War. To develop the virus, I had to understand your biology."

Dingo puffed and sat down.

"What the hell is going on in here?" Martinez demanded as he came out of the kitchen. "It felt like an earthquake."

"I'm sorry, Sheriff," I said. "Dingo was giving a lesson in hand-to-hand, human versus Enochian."

"That would be useful," Martinez said, considering the idea, but shook his head. "We don't have time right now. Anyway, I'm surprised my wife didn't come back in here and take down the both of you." He looked at Dingo and me. "She would have, if you had awakened the kid. You'd rather fight me. Believe me."

He glanced at all three of us. "I'm on my way to the Enochian Reservation. This is your last chance to back out." Dingo, Denise, and I got up. Martinez shook his head and said, "Come on."

On the way out of town, we met an ambulance at the Sheriff's Office. I could see two Native Americans sitting in the front of the vehicle. There might have been more in the back, but I couldn't be sure. Both wore grim expressions, expecting some type of trouble. I hoped their expectations were wrong.

They nodded to us as we pulled up and motioned for Martinez to drive ahead of them. The rider on the passenger side had a metal tube sticking up between his legs. It was a .50-caliber semi-automatic rifle, government-issue at the time of the War. They were supposed to have been turned in to the Army when the War was over. I didn't mention the weapon to anyone as we drove the eighteen miles down Highway 70 toward Tularosa, the last human enclave before we entered the Enochian Reservation.

No one spoke on the way to Tularosa. The dark New Mexico night flowed by the windows of the truck as we rode toward the Enochian Reservation. The lights of Tularosa seemed to bring Denise out of her deep thought.

"Tularosa hasn't changed since I was here six years ago," Denise said. "Why haven't they benefitted from Enochian trade?"

Martinez answered her, but I could tell that his mind was on the teenagers. "The Tularosan council decided to have nothing to do with the Enochians." He shrugged his shoulders. "Aliens are not allowed inside the town at all. It seems that if there were going to be problems with the Enochians, it would have been with this town, not with the Apaches." Martinez sounded petulant as he spoke. I saw the sheriff sigh in the passing lights of the town.

Martinez pulled the truck to the side of the road and waited for the ambulance to pull up beside us. He told them not to obstruct any search that the Enochians decided they needed to do. The passenger still had the rifle between his legs. Martinez noticed.

"Put that damn rifle up," he said. "If they want to confiscate it, give it to them. And don't give them any flack over it." The passenger nodded, but he didn't seem to like the order. Martinez pulled back onto the highway and headed for the Enochian border.

After about a mile, floodlights and a twenty-foot-high barbed-wire fence came into view. More lights and another fence sat about fifty feet beyond that. Martinez stopped on the Tularosa side of the line and talked with two police officers from the town.

"Hey Joe," one of the officers said. "Why you going onto the Enochian Reservation?"

"I've got three casualties on the other side, Mario," Martinez said, with a bit of irritation in his voice. "Open that damn gate, so I can get through."

"Those things kill three of your people?"

"Mario, open the damn gate," Martinez demanded.

"All right, don't bite my head off," Mario said, as he went inside the guardhouse.

"Mario," Martinez yelled, "I'll tell you about it later."

The officer nodded and waved as the gate opened. Martinez drove the truck through, with the ambulance following us. He stopped the truck about five feet before the second gate, which led to the Enochian Reservation. A tall, blue figure walked out of the guardhouse toward the sheriff's truck. Martinez had kept the window down. I shivered through my light jacket. My hands were almost as blue as the alien that approached us.

"Sheriff Martinez," the alien said with the slight accent of those Enochians accustomed to human speech. "My name is Vega and I was sent—" Vega cut off abruptly and stared momentarily at Dingo, and then he clicked and whistled at Dingo.

"He's challenging Dingo to come up with identification," Denise said, whispering to me. My body tensed slightly for trouble. My mind remembered the rifle in the ambulance behind us. Denise put her hand on my arm and shook her head.

Martinez spoke before Dingo could react.

"Look," the sheriff said, anger tingeing his voice slightly, "I've got three dead boys on the reservation somewhere. Because of that, there are some extremely angry and upset people back home. I don't have time for your petty political or social bullshit." Martinez had never raised his voice, but Vega took a step back from the verbal blast he had received.

The alien glared at Martinez and then Dingo. He glanced into the back seat. "Sheriff, who are these people and who is the strange Enochian?"

"These three have business with Rivera that is none of your concern," Martinez snapped, speaking with an authority that seemed to come naturally to him. "Gintomen can deal with them. I would bet that your orders are to bring me to the dead Apache children as quickly as you can. I suggest that you do that, now."

Vega hesitated before opening the back door and scrunching into the seat behind the sheriff, beside Denise. I made a bet to myself that Martinez was a sergeant during the War.

Vega smelled of anger and musk. I had gotten used to Dingo's smell, but the addition of one more Enochian into the close quarters of the truck was almost too much to bear. Despite the cold, I rolled the window down a couple of inches. Denise leaned closer to me. She had been away from the smell for a few years.

I was surprised that the other two guards at the scene did not search the ambulance. But when Vega settled in, he gave directions to Martinez. The bodies had been moved to the headquarters and residence for Rivera, the Rejected Prefect of the Enochians.

The next twenty minutes passed in silence as Martinez drove. I felt as if I was leaving the Earth and going to a strange world, quite different from my own. Intellectually, I knew I was still in New Mexico on what used to be the White Sands Missile Range. Emotionally, I felt completely isolated from the rest of humanity, except for Denise, who clung to my side to get away from Vega's smell. Even Martinez seemed almost alien to me as we drove to the Prefect's residence.

When we arrived at the building, my sense of isolation increased. The structure was unlike that of a human building. Curves and angles appeared in the design that were different from the way a human architect would have laid out the plans. It was very alien in structure and esthetics. I thought the building was compelling, but ugly.

We stopped at a gate, but passed through with a click and whistle from Vega. Denise leaned closer and whispered to me that security had never been this tight when she had lived here. When Martinez stopped the truck, Vega jumped out and hurried into the building without a word to us. We fell out of the truck and I stretched my muscles. I was tired and irritable, though I tried to hide it. I motioned for Denise to come over to where I was standing. Martinez and Dingo were on the other side of the truck, discussing whether we should follow Vega inside.

"What did you mean that security wasn't this tight when you lived here?" I asked Denise.

"This building was open to the public," she said. "That fence is new. I have a bad feeling about it, that's all."

I understood what she was talking about. Martinez motioned for us to follow them inside. As we got to the door, Vega and another Enochian stepped out to greet us.

"Gintomen," Martinez said. "Under different circumstances, it would be good to see you." The sheriff offered his hand. Gintomen took it and muttered a greeting. He barely looked at the sheriff. I heard a click and a whistle that sounded much the same as when Kristen, Denise's daughter, had pronounced Dingo's Enochian name back in Midland. Dingo responded. I leaned over to Denise.

"Gintomen knows him," I said. "He knows Dingo's name."

Denise nodded as the two Enochians spoke to one another. She translated, loosely. "Dingo has told him that he and the two of us have business on the reservation of the utmost importance." Gintomen responded and Denise stopped to listen. "Gintomen wants to know the nature of the visit."

"You can do that shit later," Martinez barked. Five heads, two human and three Enochian, turned toward him. "I want the bodies of our children and all the evidence that you have gathered about their murders."

"Sheriff, those deaths took place on the Enochian Reservation," Gintomen said. "The deaths are outside your jurisdiction."

Martinez stepped between Dingo and the Enochian security chief and brought his face and body as close to Gintomen as he could. He spoke in low tones, but with a force that was hard to describe. "Gintomen, we have been friends for a long time, though I can't tell it from talking to you tonight. If you do not take me to the bodies of those children murdered on your reservation, then you and I will have a lot of talking to do."

I heard a click as Martinez took the safety off his gun. A louder noise behind me caught my attention. I didn't turn around. I remembered the sound of a .50-caliber rifle being readied for firing. I saw movement on both sides of my peripheral vision. The objects moving were big, but far away. There were more Enochians outside the building than could be seen. *We'll never get out of here alive, if these guys try to re-fight the OK Corral,* I thought. I stepped forward next to Dingo.

"Excuse me, sir," I said to Gintomen. "Our business is important, but I believe that the death of the three Apache teens could be related to the reason we are here."

"Stay out of this, Stimson," Martinez warned me,

without taking his glare off Gintomen. I stood my ground. Gintomen did not seem to hear me.

"Let us discuss this problem inside," I said. Gintomen turned to me. Up close, I recognized him. I knew this Enochian. I cringed as I realized that he had recognized me, too. Gintomen grinned.

"I am specimen seven hundred and eighty-nine, Captain Roger Stimson," Gintomen said. "I see that you do remember me." He puffed once and turned to Martinez. "Come on, Joe," he said, a measure of warmth returning to his voice. "You do not keep the best of company, do you?"

Gintomen turned and stomped inside the building. Vega, Dingo, and Denise followed him. I looked around. I could not see the Enochians in the shadows, but I knew they were there. I also knew their weapons were no longer pointed at us. I sighed and followed Martinez into the building, trying to calm my nerves.

20

Martinez and I caught up with the rest of the group outside of a stairwell. Gintomen looked at me hard, studying the changes on my face. I studied him just as hard, determined not to back down under the stare of the Enochian security chief. He turned away from me and opened the door. The others started down the stairs, following Vega. As I walked through the door, Gintomen grabbed my arm and stopped me.

"Actually, Captain Stimson, I am glad you are here," Gintomen said. I could not detect sarcasm in his voice, but he had not dealt with humans as much as Dingo had. Dingo had learned to imitate human emotional patterns in his speech, a talent that Gintomen lacked, making it more difficult to read clues from his speech. Gintomen turned to walk down the steps with me. I watched my feet as I descended, as the steps were wider than a human stairwell, made for Enochians. Gintomen walked slower, allowing the others to move father ahead of us. "We have had some unexplained deaths among Enochians lately," he said, watching me for a reaction.

I did not respond to his statement. When we reached the landing, Gintomen grabbed my arm again. His grip went around my arm, almost cutting off the circulation to my left hand.

"Stimson, our scientists find a correlation in the recent deaths and your unholy concoction," Gintomen said. "How many plagues did you get from your experiments on us?"

I looked up at him. In his voice and on his face I could see fear. I had learned to read the fear of the Enochian during the War. I sighed and looked away. *He thinks I've released another virus.*

"Please let go of my arm," I said, not showing emotion. Gintomen complied, but kept his gaze centered between my eyes. He wanted answers and I could not blame him. Maybe I could help. "Do you have the bodies in the morgue?"

"You did not answer me," he said.

I took a deep breath and grimaced. "My department developed two versions of the virus," I said in even tones, trying to keep my emotions in check. On the inside, I was shaking. On the outside, I hoped I hid my guilt and discomfort with the subject. "The one we released was made from a virus living harmlessly within your systems. It was developed to take advantage of a genetic abnormality we found common to your species. You received the antidote for that one."

Gintomen puffed. This was information he already knew. He wanted to know about the other avenues of our research.

"Hey," Dingo said. His voice echoed up the stairs. "You guys coming or not?"

I looked at Gintomen. "Give us a minute," I said, never taking my eyes off the Enochian in front of me. "A second virus was made with an Earth-based virus Enochians had shown some susceptibility to—herpes. As far as anything that might have been developed since I left the military . . ." I said, letting the sentence hang in the air. I accented the statement with a shrug. "Well, the government has had eight years to come up with some real killers."

Gintomen grunted and stalked down the stairs ahead of

me. I followed, picking my steps carefully and keeping an eye on the alien. Gintomen did not like me. I was responsible for most of the non-combat scars on his body. When I reached the bottom of the stairs, Dingo and Denise were waiting beside the open door to the basement.

"What's going on?" Denise asked.

I shook my head and walked past them into the hall. Martinez was entering a door about one hundred yards down the hall on the left. I followed him, with Dingo and Denise trailing me. I heard them talking in muted clicks and whistles. I walked into the Enochian morgue and was overwhelmed by the smell of Enochian bodies.

During the War, we always said that the only thing that smelled worse than an Enochian was a dead Enochian, though at the time dead Enochians were preferable to most of us military types. It meant one less alien to kill and one less Enochian that was trying to kill us.

The room was about six thousand square feet, with stretchers in rows about four feet apart. Every stretcher contained a body. There must have been a couple of hundred bodies in that room. I wondered how many of these deaths were attributed to a new virus strain. My feelings on the subject were not good.

Everyone was silent for a moment. I looked at Denise. She showed no surprise at the number of bodies in the room. I found that discomforting for some reason. It was as if she knew what was there before she went inside. She grimaced as she looked around.

I walked closer to her and whispered, "Do they keep their bodies long before disposal?" She shook her head and moved away from me.

"Where are the Apache children?" Martinez spoke through a handkerchief he had put to his face. Gintomen clicked and whistled, and two attendants bounded across tables to find the human bodies. I started to walk toward Gintomen, but Dingo grabbed my arm.

Bending down to whisper in my ear, he said, "Let Joe and Gintomen get the unpleasantness over with first. They are friends who are becoming adversaries." I must have looked blank, because Dingo puffed. "Gintomen is in an awkward situation, dealing with his pride. And Joe knows it, so he is being quite formal for the benefit of his old friend."

"You mean that I butted in outside." I started to explain that we were outnumbered about fifty to one, but Dingo puffed.

"If you had not stepped in to avert a disaster, then I would have," he said. "That was a dangerous situation. This is not."

I nodded and Dingo let go of my arm. I noticed that Denise was not watching the situation, having seen it before, and perhaps having played one of the roles in the pride drama while she lived here. She sneaked a look under a sheet that contained an Enochian body. For the first time, surprise showed in her features. She looked up, saw me, and motioned to me to come over.

She lifted the sheet for me. I was surprised, too. The Enochians had shown a susceptibility to the herpes zoster viruses when we had experimented on them during the War. The dead alien lying under the sheet had pockmarks and sores that had been runny when he was alive. I looked at Denise. "Is that the second virus you guys were working on?" She hissed the question in my ear.

"No," I whispered back. "But it could be a derivative." Before I could say anything else, the Enochian attendants returned with the three human bodies for Martinez's inspection. I grabbed Denise's arm and we moved closer to the gurneys. I knew that I needed to look at the bodies to confirm some suspicions I had begun to form about the killings.

Gintomen motioned for the attendants to pull back the sheets from the bodies. "Two of the three died instantly from one gunshot wound to the back of the neck," he said to Martinez.

The sheriff examined the bodies with an air of detachment. I had seen that type of reaction in people, especially in those who are inundated with the nasty side of life. Detachment was common in the emergency room. Sometimes, you just don't want to feel. You need the detachment to be able to do your job. I can't remember how many times I'd cried days after working on a dying child. The smallest thing could set off the emotions and horror, but at the time you witnessed the most horrible details of life, things that most people would rather not see, you distanced yourself from the humanity and dealt with the facts of the job. A human being becomes a body or a body part, not a flesh and blood being. They become problems that must be fixed.

I looked at the children on the gurneys. Through everything, you never get used to the senseless death of the young.

"What about the other child?" Martinez talked slowly, in low tones. I moved closer to the bodies.

"He bled to death slowly," Gintomen said, matter-of-factly.

I studied the children. None of the three looked over sixteen. Their bodies had taken on the ashen hue of all the dead. Eyes gazed at the ceiling without seeing. Three mothers would be mourning their sons tonight, but if what I suspected had happened turned out to be the truth, many more mothers would be grieving, soon. The smell of the

Enochian dead reentered my consciousness. *Many more mothers are already grieving,* I thought.

"Where are the entrance wounds?" I asked, staring at the child who bled to death, imagining his fear and pain.

Gintomen turned to look at me and puffed his jowls. He clicked and whistled at the attendants, who turned over the body of the one who had died slowly.

"Hmm," I said, bending down to get a better look at the wound. "No exit wound on the front. It looks like the bullet traveled up the spine into the brain."

I straightened and glanced at Denise. "It's a ritualistic killing, isn't it, Denise?"

"Yeah, it's pretty obvious, even to us," Denise said, sadly. She was about to have to pick sides and she did not like it. "Enochians killed these kids."

"Or someone wants us to think it was Enochians," Martinez said. The sheriff looked at me. "Captain Stimson, did you ever know an Enochian to not make sure their victim was dead?"

I considered what he had said. Many of the Enochians in our prison experimental medicine camp were killed for fraternization in a ritualistic manner. They only had one wound and it was a clean kill. The only time the first wound had not been a clean kill was when a wounded Enochian with limited use of his arms had to perform the ritual twice to get it right. He had not let the victim bleed to death. Another thought occurred to me, which I shared with the others.

"I've never known an Enochian to use ritualistic methods to kill a human," I said. "If anything, an Enochian would have just shot them in the head, not made a production of it." I stared at the body. "Even then, an alien wouldn't let them bleed to death. Enochians are nice, clean killers. Humans are the messy ones."

"You're right, Roger," Denise said, nodding. "Even to make a point, an Enochian would not use this method to kill anything other than another Enochian."

Dingo puffed, loudly. "I'm glad you came to those conclusions, human friends. I was about to get a bit angry if you had not." He puffed, then clicked and whistled. Gintomen whistled his agreement. Denise nodded.

"He was a butcher," Denise said to no one.

"So we're looking for humans," Martinez said. I saw relief and anger mixing on his face.

"Most definitely, old friend," Gintomen said to the sheriff. "I'm sorry I could not tell you. You had to come to this conclusion yourself."

"I've got people back home who are ready to march onto the Enochian Reservation and burn the lot of you out of here," Martinez said.

"This is only one part of the puzzle." Everyone turned to look at Dingo. "Certainly humans murdered the young ones, trying to make it look like Enochians." He looked at each of us and then turned around with his left arm stretched out toward the rest of the morgue that contained about two hundred Enochian dead. "And humans have unleashed another virus on Enochians."

"But why would anyone go to this much trouble to . . ." Denise let her words trail off. "The Sons of Earth." She twisted the end of her hair around her finger, thinking. "Sheriff, there used to be a large Sons of Earth contingent in Tularosa."

"Yeah," Martinez answered, "that's why Enochians weren't allowed in their town." He scratched his head and turned away from the bodies of the children. "I thought it folded up about four years ago."

"It did," Gintomen said. "According to our records, the

Tularosa organization ceased to exist at that time, but many members of the Sons of Earth settled in Tularosa."

I realized they were all forgetting one thing. "I agree that the Sons of Earth are probably behind this," I said, as they all turned to face me. "But they had Enochian help."

Dingo clicked and whistled at Gintomen, who straightened his body. The Enochian security chief answered him and turned to me. "Captain Stimson, you are revered on Enoch and by many on this reservation as a formidable enemy." Gintomen puffed at me. "I have my doubts that you are as formidable as my culture seems to believe—that is our way—but I do know that you are a biological weapons expert."

I held up a hand for him to stop. "Gintomen, I am honored by Enochian culture, but I was a soldier doing my duty as I saw it." I glanced around the morgue at the hundreds of Enochians lying on slabs. Guilt for my actions on the virus tried to invade my mind, but I pushed it back down. This time I could make a positive statement. "As I told you before, we were working on another virus based on an Earth organism that Enochians showed some susceptibility to."

I turned to Denise. "Kristen was about eight when you came to the reservation, correct?" She nodded. "Had she contracted chicken pox by that time?" I was answered with another nod. "That's how you recognized what these Enochians had died from." I turned to Gintomen.

"Chicken pox?" Dingo sounded confused. "But I've been among humans for the last six years, so I'm sure I've been exposed to that."

"But not to this strain, Dingo," I said. "This strain of the common childhood disease has been altered to affect Enochians, not humans, of this I'm sure. Whoever carried on Bio-Chem's work after the War would want something harmless to humans. Something as simple as the herpes virus could kill your entire civilization."

"How did it get onto the reservation?" Gintomen would be interested in the security aspects of the situation.

"My guess is it was carried in and released," I said. "Where did these deaths occur?"

"These bodies were found in the Northwest quadrant of the reservation, up in the Sacramento Mountains," Gintomen said. "An entire village died."

"This form of the human herpes zoster virus incubates for about two weeks before the disease begins. They wouldn't have changed much in the way of vectors and incubation during the virus production, I don't think." I stopped abruptly; I had a hunch. "Has the reservation been visited by human delegations in the last two weeks?"

"Only one," Gintomen answered. "It was headed by a senator from Louisiana, I think."

I sighed. It was coming together in my head, now. "Was that senator's name Boudreau? Rafe Boudreau?"

"Yes," Gintomen said. "We did a complete background check on the senator. I know that he has not been friendly to the Enochians in his congressional votes, but his record is impeccable."

"You probably should have checked him out more thoroughly, Gintomen," I said as I nodded to myself. I looked up to see all of their eyes on me. "Boudreau was the general who oversaw the Bio-Chem lab I ran during the War. I reported to him."

21

"You think a Louisiana senator is responsible for the murder of two hundred Enochians," Martinez said, with an eyebrow cocked.

"Boudreau, along with one of his henchmen, came to see me after Dingo came into the emergency room," I said. "He tried to recruit me first, but I told him I wasn't interested. He left with a veiled threat about 'doing things the hard way.' "

Martinez scratched his head. "I'm not sure that a veiled threat constitutes proof, Mr. Stimson."

"My apartment became a bit airy afterwards," I said. "The night of his visit, I began losing friends and colleagues at an alarming rate. I'm afraid a police detective in New Orleans was their last victim. It may not be proof, but it's sure as hell coincidental and I don't believe in coincidence."

"Boudreau is a possible candidate for president, isn't he?" Dingo asked as he stroked a jowl.

I shrugged. "A flare-up with the Enochians gives Boudreau even more motive. If Gamble works out a real peace with the Enochians, then the opposition ought to just fold." I grinned at Dingo. "I've seen the type of technology that Enochians have that can be adapted to human use."

"How do you propose to prove that Senator Boudreau had anything to do with the death of the Enochians on this reservation?" Martinez asked in a monotone. I could tell that he was angry by the tautness on his face. "Anything we have now looks extremely circumstantial."

"I don't plan on exposing Boudreau," I said. "I wish I

165

could, but Boudreau will be insulated from the entire affair." I looked at Gintomen, who nodded in a human
fashion. Maybe he had been around more humans than I
first thought. "Boudreau was the one responsible for my
ability to release the first virus without approval from Command HQ. I insulated him during the War, and the bastard
tried to have me sent to prison."

Silence filled the morgue for a few seconds. Martinez
spoke quietly to Gintomen. "We need to keep our peoples
from going to war, old friend."

Gintomen nodded his agreement and then turned to me.
"Stimson, will you help our people to isolate an agent that
will kill your new virus?" The use of the word "your"
touched on my feelings of guilt. Enochians have learned a
lot about human psychology since the end of the War. I
agreed, and watched the two lawmen walk out of the room.

"I have some things to do," Dingo said to me.

"I'm going with him," Denise said, quickly. "I can't
stand this smell." Denise's reminder of the smell around me
filled my nostrils with the aroma of Enochian dead. I wondered how I became accustomed to it so quickly.

"And how am I going to communicate with these guys?"
I said, glancing in the direction of the techs.

"You'll get along," Dingo said. He turned and left the
morgue in a hurry. Denise followed him. I walked toward
the techs and asked them if they had cultures of the virus.
The one closest to me answered in English and showed me
to the microbiology lab.

I quickly found out that one of the attendants was an
Enochian exobiologist, studying Earth-based microbes.
They had isolated the virus soon after the first victim had
been found. Measures had been taken to limit the spread by
quarantining an entire section of the old White Sands

National Park. Achieving their objective trumped any other concerns the Enochians had, like freedom of movement for the affected populations. The quarantine had come too late for the two hundred and thirty-three who lay dead in the morgue, but it had contained the outbreak.

Borgias, the exobiologist, explained the procedures of the lab and did all of the tests I asked him to perform. I had been right. The virus was one of the herpes strains we had been developing when we discovered the Enochians' own plague residing in their bodies. The varicella strain had been genetically altered to attach to an Enochian host and produce a lethal form of chicken pox.

"The old chicken pox vaccine, modified for Enochians, should do the trick," I said, looking at the literature on the vaccine on the computer. "What do you think, Borgias?"

The Enochian grunted and said, "We can do that here in the lab, as long as the human government will allow us to have the vaccine."

I looked at the scientist. There was a graying around his jowls, and the blue hue of a younger Enochian's skin looked rather lighter, almost grayish, on Borgias. I could not read his body language, but I could understand his uncertainty and mistrust of humans.

I noticed a small white scar on his left arm, slightly above the elbow, which had been hidden by an old-fashioned lab coat. I recognized that scar as the same as one that Gintomen had. I was responsible for his mistrust of humans. Borgias had not shown any inclination of doubt or mistrust toward me, though he knew who I was. Perhaps it was because I was the "formidable enemy," but I did not think that was the reason. Enochians were naturally polite to one another, I guess to avoid an injury to pride. That politeness extended to all their contacts, even humans.

"Borgias, our people are not at war," I said, "and the government will not interfere in a private transaction. The drug company will have that order on the plane by Monday morning." The old Enochian puffed in response. I might have puffed myself, if I had jowls with which to puff. My words sounded as hollow to me as I'm sure they sounded to him. There was no mistaking that a human had set this virus on the Enochian Reservation. I heard a chirping sound, and Borgias got up from the computer station.

I leaned forward, resting my elbows on the desk, and rubbed my eyes, exhausted from lack of sleep. Fatigue settled into my body. I did not think about anything except wanting to be home in my own bed, even if I did have a number of large holes in my living room and my kitchen and my bedroom. I wondered if my landlord was going to evict me when I got back to New Orleans. I'd be working a lot of overtime to pay for the damages. Did insurance cover damages from attempted murder? I shook my head to clear away the inane thoughts. Borgias startled me back to the present.

"Your presence is requested elsewhere," he said. "I will have an assistant guide you."

I nodded and got up from the desk. Borgias thanked me for my help and left. He bowed as he left. I sat back down, alone in the lab. Fatigue returned and I rubbed my eyes again. Something not quite right nagged at my brain. From the involvement of my old commanding officer, to Denise's easy acceptance of the fact that more than two hundred Enochians lay dead on slabs in the morgue in the next room. Things did not fit.

The Enochians I had encountered on this trip were more than they seemed. What was an exobiologist doing as a reject? Did I really know enough about Enochian society? Dingo had insisted that he had to get to the reservation and pick up Denise. Dingo had facets about him that seemed to grow every time he opened his mouth. I couldn't see him as an anthropologist or a salesman. Dingo gathered intelligence for one reason or another. I just didn't know for what reason.

And then there was Denise. Eminent—though disgraced by her previous association with the Sons of Earth—anthropologist Denise Windham held an air of coolness about her. I began to wonder if she had orchestrated the whole affair, right down to the supposed assassination of the U.S. President. I shook my head. How many of these suspicions were the result of fatigue and paranoia? I wasn't sure. The only thing I was sure about was that the answers to my particular problems were not here in New Mexico. My answers would be found on Canal Street on Monday morning, in the form of a small alien by the name of Rafta.

"Excuse me, sir." I looked up to see a young Enochian at the door. "I have been ordered to show you to the Security Sector. Will you follow me?" I sighed. The Enochian sounded like a private talking to an important guest. Hell, all the Enochians here sounded like they were in the military, and that struck another sour note in my mind. "Sir," the Enochian insisted, "I was told that it was urgent that you be taken there."

I got up and followed the Enochian out of the room. My thoughts and suspicions went with me, just under the edges of my conscious mind. I wasn't ready to trust anyone at this moment, not even Denise. "Maybe especially not Denise," I said under my breath. I just had to follow through with the events that had been put into motion. The younger Enochian said nothing as he led me down the pristine white halls of the Enochian compound. What could be urgent, when everything had been at a frantic pace? I wasn't sure I wanted to know.

22

Dingo filled me in on the research he and Denise performed while I was isolating the Enochian strain of chicken pox. I half-listened, noticing that Gintomen, Martinez, and Denise were in discussions within the same room as Dingo and I, but I could not catch the conversation. My eyes gravitated toward the activity in the next room, separated from us by a glass partition.

I understood why the halls of the Enochian complex had been so deserted while we had walked through them. Every alien in the place seemed to be in the next room. Well, at least seventy-five of them were working in a command room, the type you used to see when movies depicted scenes inside the Pentagon, or in the old war movies. A map of the Enochian Reservation was electronically displayed in the center portion of the room in three-dimensional detail. Certain areas of that map were shaded in red. The building we were in, and the small community surrounding it, was a white island in a sea of red. Most of the other areas on the reservation were white, except for a small area in the northwest quadrant. Evidently, the Enochians were monitoring activities that were currently happening on the reservation. The scene in the command room cemented my impression of the general martial nature of the Enochian presence in New Mexico.

"What?" I asked. Dingo's words did not register in my mind. The alien puffed his jowls twice in disgust, then clicked and whistled at me, an angry whistle if I ever heard one. I raised an eyebrow and said to him, "And you're a worse one." Dingo stopped talking and looked at me as if I had lost my mind. He changed to English, calming his voice as he did.

"Rafta does not exist as far as Enochians are concerned," Dingo said. "No one has ever erased themselves from the master computer files. No one."

"Dingo, you said yourself that you did not exist in those files," I said. Dingo shot a look at Gintomen, who was sitting across the large outer room of the security sector, talking excitedly to Denise and Martinez. I wanted to know what they were discussing, but I had not been invited to take part in their conversation. Dingo had grabbed me as I walked in the door. And then there was the command center taking some of my attention.

"I lied," Dingo said, turning his gaze toward me. "What Rafta has done is not only impossible, but highly illegal for an Enochian. It's like desertion in your armed forces. Or being a traitor."

I had not turned my attention back to Dingo. I was studying Denise. She looked upset. I thought I saw tears running down her face. Dingo noticed where my attention had wandered and puffed.

"That's the main reason we sent for you," Dingo said. I raised an eyebrow, but otherwise didn't respond. I studied the three beings in hot discussion across the room. Dingo told me anyway. I knew he would. "About five minutes ago, my cell phone rang with a call for Denise. I lied and said that she was not with me."

"What did they say?"

"They told me to have Denise near the phone in five minutes or her daughter would be killed."

"Aw, shit." I thought of young Kristen, who had been so damned curious about Dingo. I suspected that they had brought Rafta to coax her away from her friend's house. Kristen trusted all Enochians. She had no reason not to trust them. I nodded toward Denise, Martinez, and Gintomen. "What are they doing?"

"Gintomen is explaining how he will trace the call and plant a transmitter into the caller's cell phone."

"Plant a transmitter?" I didn't understand what Dingo was telling me. I asked him how Gintomen could plant a bug on a phone without physically going to the phone in question. "Is this advanced Enochian technology?" I was surprised by the blank look on Dingo's face.

"No, we received this in trade with your government," Dingo said evenly. "This is a human technology."

I whistled at the implications of that answer. How much spying can the Feds do on their own citizenry? God, how much did they know about me? *What am I thinking? Everybody knows everything about me, or so it seems.*

"Do we have any idea who grabbed Kristen?" I asked the question, despite having my own suspicions. The Sons of Earth seemed too involved in my own troubles. It was the type of terror operation that fool Williams would try. *How does Boudreau fit into this?* Answers eluded me.

Dingo puffed. "They did not identify themselves. But I think we both know."

I nodded and walked toward the others, noticing that Dingo followed me. I wondered if they had wanted to get their stories straight before I got there. But Martinez was there, and I didn't suspect his motives in this adventure. I only mistrusted the Enochians, for some reason I could not put my finger on, and Denise. I wanted to know her involvement in this escapade. My schoolboy crush was as strong as it ever had been, when I looked at her. I tried to tell myself that my suspicions were all fatigue-induced paranoia, but I could not convince myself. The Enochians were hiding something on their reservation. The other three acknowledged me, but stopped talking.

Gintomen asked if Dingo had brought me up to date on the kidnapping of Denise's daughter. I nodded. A question formed in my mind and I turned to Dingo.

"You said Rafta did not exist on the master computer files," I began. "Does that mean that Rafta has disappeared entirely from all Enochian records?"

"Yes, and it is quite disconcerting because they always keep such control over—" Gintomen interrupted Dingo with a fierce click and whistle. Dingo bowed slightly, and shut up.

I turned to the Enochian security chief. "You have access to the homeworld records don't you?" I asked, speaking softly, but firmly.

Gintomen did not respond. I exploded with a few words that I thought I had forgotten. Gintomen's heritage, as well as that of the Enochian Prefect, came into question during the next few seconds of my outrage. The insults held no meaning for the Enochians, since they did not recognize the idea of bastardy. Nor were they especially concerned that their mothers were compared to dogs. I stopped and caught my breath.

Dingo opened his mouth to speak, but I thundered at him. "I'm not talking to you!" I screamed at Dingo. "I'm going to talk to your goddamned commanding officer."

I glared at Gintomen. He puffed at me twice. An air of indifference exuded from his posture and eyes. I tried to control my anger. "This has been an Enochian operation all along, hasn't it?"

Gintomen did not respond. I felt that I was running on dangerous ground, but I did not care. If Gintomen wanted to challenge me, I would accept. *My coworkers are dead and people tried to kill me, damn it!* my mind screamed. But when I spoke, my voice was controlled, though I felt heat around my face and neck.

"I want the truth," I said to Gintomen. "Was this 'reservation' always a military outpost for the Enochians?"

"Roger, it doesn't matter," Denise said. "They are our friends."

For a moment, I forgot the anguish she was feeling. "Your 'friends' don't lie to you," I said. My voice stayed a couple of decibels below a scream. "No one's been straight with me, since I started on this escapade. Even the lies Dingo told at Martinez's house did not stand up under scrutiny. It seems to me that the whole damn thing had been orchestrated for my benefit."

The look of hurt on her face surprised me, and I regretted my outburst. Did I cause her that pain, or was it worry for her daughter?

"I haven't lied to you, Roger, though I may have misled you a bit," Denise whispered. "Someone *is* trying to kill the President and the Prefect, and the Enochians needed your help. You owed them. You said so yourself." Her eyes, swollen by crying over her daughter, held a fierce look in them that I had not seen before. "Those bastards, the Sons of Earth, have my baby. And they're the ones trying to restart this war, not the Enochians."

I reached down to hug her and tell her that we would get Kristen back, but she threw off my arms and stepped back, dislodging a desk from its moorings.

"Your sanctimonious guilt about having killed so many Enochians has been around your neck for so long, and yet you forget it when you find that the aliens have kept an intelligence base on a planet to watch over a culture that almost annihilated them.

"You wasted all those years grieving for your wife and for the billions of Enochians you killed," she continued, her voice coming under a bit more control. "They shouldn't have tried to court-martial you for releasing the virus. They should have given you the Medal of Honor." She hesitated and took a deep breath. When she spoke again, her tone was less harsh, almost professionally therapeutic. "If you hadn't unleashed that virus and nearly wiped them out, they would have destroyed Earth."

"What? But I thought you said . . ." I stopped. I was confused and disoriented.

Denise walked up to me and put a hand on my arm, and my anger vanished. I realized that what I felt for this woman I had known for less than a day was more than a crush. "Believe me, Roger, without the release of the virus, we wouldn't exist anymore."

I looked into her eyes and saw the pain she was experiencing. I wanted to ask her what she was talking about, but my mind began to think of Kristen, her daughter. I would do whatever I could to help Denise get her daughter from those people.

"I've got a million questions, but getting Kristen back safely is paramount," I said. "Stopping the onset of another war with the Enochians is more important too. We would not survive this one, would we?" Denise shook her head.

"Like you almost did not survive the last one," said a voice from behind me. "Captain Stimson, I have wanted to meet you for a long time." I turned to look at an old Enochian woman, flanked by an entourage of armed Enochian soldiers. She was dressed in a golden tunic, much different from the ones Dingo and Gintomen wore. "You killed my mate and two of my children," she said without malice.

I realized that she was the Prefect of the Rejected.

23

The armed guards took up defensive positions around the room and, though they didn't aim their weapons at me, I knew that I was the only threat they perceived at the moment. The Prefect of the Rejected studied me as one might a drunken Enochian in the emergency room. I studied her back.

What I saw was an old Enochian female. I knew that she was old from the whiteness of her jowls. Her forehead was a bit higher than that of her male companions and she held her head in a regal manner. She was accustomed to her authority. Her skin had not faded like that of the old microbiologist, but she had not been defeated as he had. The Prefect had not been on Earth during the War. She had not seen the destruction of her army firsthand. I was speculating, but it made sense, and the speculation supported my observation that the Enochian Reservation was actually a military outpost.

Why would they need a military outpost? *They may want to keep us contained in our own solar system while they decide what to do with us,* I thought. The old Enochian turned to the others. Dingo and Gintomen stood rigidly at attention. Martinez had risen from his chair and bowed his head toward her as he stood at ease, like the old soldier that he was.

"Denise, it is good to see you once again," she said. "But I wish it was under better circumstances. I trust that Gintomen is helping you find your daughter." The Prefect cast a quick look at the security chief; Gintomen did not move or acknowledge her glance.

"Thank you, Rivera," Denise said, an amount of deference in her voice. "Everything that can be done is being done. You know Captain Roger Stimson, late of the U.S. Army Intelligence Biological and Chemical Warfare Unit, but I would like the honor of formally introducing you to him." She grabbed my arm and we took a step toward Rivera. I glanced at the guards, who stiffened at our movement. Denise ignored them.

"Roger, this is Rivera, Prefect of the Rejected on Earth."

I nodded at her in the same manner as Martinez. I was most decidedly not at ease, due to her statement about my killing her mate and two children. I knew that was meant to throw me off-guard. It worked to a great degree. However, I took a chance when I spoke to her.

"And you are the Enochian Prefect's representative, am I correct, ma'am?"

She puffed a white jowl in my direction, but otherwise ignored my question. I could hear Dingo clicking and whistling under his breath. Rivera turned to him, clicking and whistling. I was surprised that Dingo did not back down; his answer was just as fierce. She waved an arm at him, which ended the conversation, though I heard Dingo still swearing in his language. She turned and looked at the map in the other room.

"Gintomen, have you heard from the advance force?" Rivera asked in English. She wanted us to know what was happening.

"They have been successful," Gintomen said. "The leader will be brought to this complex in the next few minutes."

Rivera said nothing in response, studying the red on the

map. After a few minutes, Rivera asked, "How many casualties have there been?"

"Light," Gintomen responded. Though he held an attitude of respect for Rivera, I sensed that, like Dingo, he didn't report directly to her. "Fewer than," he hesitated, making a calculation into human math, "twenty Enochians have been killed. Your policy of combative non-combativeness has worked well."

She puffed a white jowl hard. "Captain Stimson, do you know what is happening here?" Rivera didn't turn around to look at me.

I walked toward the glass partition to stand next to her. One of her guards stopped me with a weapon in my stomach. Rivera clicked once and he let me pass. I glanced at the map, noting that the red areas had not grown, but they hadn't become smaller, either. I turned toward Rivera. "You are having an uprising of some sort. Probably due to the fact that someone or some organization doesn't like the fact that Enochians and Earth will be trading partners. We hurt you too badly."

She turned to me. "That is a very perceptive observation, Captain Stimson. You did indeed hurt us badly. The virus nearly ended our race and empire," she said, glancing at Gintomen over my shoulder. "There are some, mainly in the Lanaka, who would have us sever all ties with you and destroy your world. Enochians have considered the idea." She studied me, again. Was she looking for a sign of weakness?

"You may find that harder to do than you think," I said, guarding my voice from the anger rising within me. "Our government always prepares for a possible enemy's capabilities. The key word there is 'possible.' Though we haven't been at war for eight years now, I am sure that our military has begun to apply the knowledge it learned during the War and in the time since." I thought of the Enochian bodies in the morgue below us. "And biologically, your race is still vulnerable, as we both know."

She puffed toward the glass partition. "Beyond the range of your deep space radar is an armada of ships approaching Earth with the capability to utterly destroy this planet, but it will not be used because the decision has been made to allow you to join the empire."

She turned back to the map of her domain and was silent for a moment. She spoke to me without looking. "Do you know what it means to be a part of the trading empire of the Enochians?"

I remembered what Denise had written in her book about the fairness of the system, but she had been shown what the Enochians wanted her to see. I said nothing.

"It means," Rivera continued, "being a part of a great enterprise, one that could increase your technology by hundreds of your years. And all of the partners are equal." She turned to look at me. Her eyes, voice, and manner seemed to exude a certain sadness, but with an Enochian, it could have meant resentment, hate, or any number of things.

"The Enochians have been the first among equals in that partnership for so long we cannot remember being less. I believe, and many Enochians fear, that humans may supplant us at the top of the chain in a century or two." She stared hard at the map for a moment, and then her attention turned to one of the large monitors on the left side of the command room's walls.

"They have arrived," Rivera said. "Operations like the one here are occurring all over the empire as we speak. We are ferreting out the Enochian traitors who are against your admission to that empire. They are afraid of you. They say we should have destroyed you during the War. Only the virus stopped us. You showed us that humanity could be a formidable enemy, Captain Stimson. And, according to our beliefs, a formidable enemy can turn into a formidable friend," she said, hesitating before adding, "or a living nightmare."

She pointed a long, blue finger at the map. "We are doing our part to make this admission possible, even over the objections of a strong minority of our people. You must do the rest. You must stop the assassinations on Monday. Any actions by us would be misinterpreted."

I nodded. If the Enochians were to send a large group to find a rogue Lanaka agent, humans might see it as a threat to their sovereignty. Rivera abruptly walked toward the door, her guards following, then stopped at the doorway and turned back to me. "You stopped one war, Stimson. Try to avoid another one between our species. I'm not sure either species would survive this time." Rivera stormed out; I figured she was on her way to greet her new prisoners.

I stared at the vacant doorway after the last of Rivera's guards had left. They expected me to stop an assassination that I couldn't get the U.S. government to take seriously. Did their beliefs make them think that I would have enough influence to accomplish anything?

"How the hell am I supposed to stop an organized opposition which wants to kill two leaders?" I was muttering to myself. "My government thinks I'm a murderer, and the Enochians have their hands tied and can't act."

"They believe you to be an honorable man, Roger," Denise said, looking up at me. I looked at her. "Even though they know that you have no power, they believe that you will try to stop another war." She reached out to touch my arm. "They know that you understand the consequences. They want you to show the same resolve in saving our two cultures that you once showed in trying to destroy them eight years ago."

"But I don't have the same resources now that I had then," I said, shaking my head. I pulled my arm away from her and rubbed my eyes. I was tired and I felt very alone. *Why me?* I could not answer the question, but I knew that I would try.

"You were right, Roger," Denise said. "This is a military base." I looked at her again. She hugged herself and looked as if she might break into tears again at any moment. "The signs were all right here in front of me, but I didn't want to see. This reservation, the whole idea of the Rejected, was a farce to cover their purpose of having a foothold on Earth in order to restart the War, if they felt they had to destroy us. They needed a way to keep an eye on humans without having to deal directly with them."

She took a deep breath and blew it out slowly. "I feel so used." Denise looked up at me. "I'm sorry I got you involved in this."

I nodded, but did not respond.

Denise looked away and appeared lost in thought. When she began to talk, she would not look at me. "Dingo called me a week ago and told me about the plot to kill the President and the Prefect. He asked my advice on how to get you involved in the project." She turned and gazed into my eyes. Tears welled up and escaped her eyes, rolling down her cheeks. "I'm sorry, Roger, I really am."

I wiped the tears from her face. "You did what you thought was right." I was surprised I wasn't angry, but I could not feel anger. All I could feel was fatigue. The sense of being overwhelmed pervaded my tired and guilty mind.

"You were not my first choice, Captain." Dingo had walked up behind us. "But the Prefect wanted the most well-known human to be the one to help us out of this situation." Dingo puffed at me.

I looked at Denise, gave her a quick hug. "Dingo, have we heard from them, yet?"

He shook his head. "No," he said to me, and then he turned around, leaving us alone.

Denise stayed in my embrace for a few minutes. Her shoulders moved, but she cried without sound. I think she felt as helpless and overwhelmed as I felt. I stroked her hair, but we did not talk.

Dingo cleared his throat to get our attention. "Dr. Windham, it is they." She disengaged herself from my arms and walked toward the phone.

Movement on the other side of the glass partition caught my eye. I could hear the muffled clicks and whistles of approval coming from the Enochians monitoring the small rebellion. They all gazed at one of the large monitors. I turned my head toward the picture that had aroused them.

I saw two Enochians, who could have been a part of Rivera's guard, carrying a third Enochian out of the main door to the security complex, though dragging was more like it. Someone in the control room fiddled with the picture, and a close-up of the three appeared on the screen. The alien being dragged slumped between the two guards with his head hanging limply. I saw the blue-tinged Enochian blood coming from the back of the slumped Enochian's neck. As the guards reached the door, two more aliens grinned at them and opened the facility.

The two guards dragged the third alien through the doors and, without ceremony, dumped him down the wide, long steps of the building. The alien body rolled toward the bottom of the steps, coming to rest face-up. I had known the Enochian was dead. I recognized him as the one identified as the leader of the uprising. The two guards turned away from the alien and walked back inside.

I thought about the ruthlessness with which the Enochians had put down the rebellion, but I remembered Gintomen telling Rivera that casualties had been light and that the non-combative measures had been successful. Perhaps the Enochians had been as fair as they could with a majority of the rebels, but the leaders were forced to pay the ultimate price for their disloyalty.

What would the Enochians do, if Earth were against them in a matter of the trading empire? Would they just kill off the leaders of the dissident faction and leave the others alone? My thoughts went to the long history of martyrdom on our planet. Death only validates a martyr for a cause; most of our religions proved that point. Would the Enochians truly understand humanity's need for a dead hero?

I felt someone coming up behind me. Turning, I saw that Dingo stood next to me. He leaned down to whisper in my ear. "They are calling from New Orleans."

I nodded. The aliens in the command room had become louder in their celebration. The map of the Enochian Reservation began changing from red to white, all except for the northwest quadrant. I thought about the bodies in the morgue, and I knew I had no choice. Neither Boudreau, nor Rivera and Dingo, nor Denise had pointed out to me what I had to do next.

I knew what my next destination would be on this adventure I had reluctantly taken. I glanced back at the image of the dead alien lying at the bottom of the steps and thought again of martyrdom. I turned away from the screen. *Next stop Bourbon Street,* I thought. I had unfinished business with James Williams.

24

The trip to the Enochian Reservation had not provided the essential information Dingo sought about Rafta, but it had been instructive for me. The monitor closed in on the bottom of the stairs. I stood staring at the body of the rebel faction leader. The workers in the command center dwindled to a skeletal crew as the red patches on the map shrank to one quadrant of the northwest Enochian territory. Some of the aliens had begun to gather outside of the building as the first rays of dawn filtered onto the New Mexico landscape.

One Enochian walking down the steps stopped, then looked at the camera and kicked the rebel leader in the face. I turned away from the screen, disgusted with the violent treatment. One more glance showed a succession of kicks and gouges by the victorious Enochians. The rebel leader, even if he was still alive, wouldn't live long. I turned my back to the command center and the monitor.

Had I been any better in my treatment of Enochian prisoners during the War? I knew the answer. I'd demanded that the Enochians be treated with respect, and torture was forbidden, a troublesome order since Lolich headed the guard unit. But despite my orders, hadn't I been guilty of torture, at least in the psychological sense? How many prisoners died because of my experiments? Whatever my past, I had to deal with the fact that I could not change those actions. I refocused my thoughts on the business before me and glanced around the room.

Denise had not returned. Dingo and Gintomen had

moved into a large office at the back of the security office. Martinez sat alone at a desk, staring at the monitor I tried to ignore. He winced and tried to look away, but the scene compelled his attention. I walked toward him, which gave him a reason to turn away. I saw him sigh.

"They are a violent species," Martinez said. "How brutal would they be, if Earth decided not to join their partnership?"

"I don't know, but I've been thinking along those same lines," I said. "It may be: join or die."

He nodded and turned to the screen. My eyes followed. The rebel leader lay still, little more than a bloody spot at the bottom of the steps. *They have to make an example*, I thought. Was the example for their population, to let them know what happens when you fight against the authority of the Prefect? Or were the Enochians making an example of their own dissenters for humanity? *See what we have done for you, so that you may enter our Confederation.* Another Enochian foot rocked the body. Did they do this in support of not destroying Earth? I thought about my part in this situation. I had been led by the nose until I could not get out. Dingo and Denise had made sure that I would finish what they'd started. I had few choices and none of them good. I thought about Dingo.

"What did you mean that Dingo did not exist as far as the Rejected Enochians were concerned?"

Martinez looked up and shrugged.

"Come on, Sheriff, tell me." My voice never rose, but the inflection of my words affected Martinez.

He frowned. "Stimson, you needed to know that Dingo was not what he said he was," Martinez said. "But Dingo is a good man, and I use the term inclusively, for humans and Enochians alike. If he is with the Lanaka, which I can't prove or disprove, then he would be of a faction that is out to follow the Prefect's directives." Martinez glanced at the office where the two aliens were speaking. "I have never known him or Gintomen to lie to me, Captain, though I have suspected some misleading statements in the past. I let those incidents pass, usually because they dealt with Enochian business, which was not also Apache or Mescalero business. But the one thing I do know is that Gintomen is no damn security chief."

Martinez didn't know any more than I knew, though it seemed he had the same suspicions. I nodded at the sheriff and sighed. I sat down, and we both waited for the aliens to return. And Denise. I couldn't stand to see Denise hurting. I recognized the feelings I had for her, but marveled that those feeling had stirred so soon after meeting the woman. I had never believed in love at first sight.

A loud click and whistle interrupted my thoughts. I glanced toward the room containing Dingo and Gintomen, then to Martinez, who did not open his eyes.

"They are arguing over whether you should continue to be involved in this operation," Martinez said, never looking at me. "Dingo said that you were a private citizen now, and should not have been dragged into this in the first place."

I stared at the sheriff. "How the hell di—"

Martinez waved a hand at me to be silent. "Gintomen said that your involvement had been decided at the highest levels of the Lanaka. He said that the Enochian people would expect 'Earth's greatest hero' to be a part of defusing the assassination of the Prefect."

I saw the door slam, and the discussion became muted. Martinez smiled.

"They don't know you speak their language, do they?" Martinez had already earned my respect for the way he dealt with Gintomen, but that respect grew.

Maybe he *did* know more than I knew.

The sheriff shook his head and then sighed. "Before I started translating, Gintomen stated he was not entirely pleased with the way Rivera handled the uprising," Martinez said, the smile vanishing from his face. "I suspect that our two Lanakan friends do not entirely trust the Prefect of the Rejected."

That made sense to me.

Rivera had voiced her concerns over the admission of humans to the Enochian Trading Confederation. She had also imposed a condition of nonviolence against the rebellious aliens on Gintomen, leaving the rebel factions intact, with the exception of the unfortunate Enochian dying or dead just outside the building. I glanced at the monitor. The body lay alone at the bottom of the steps.

Martinez fell silent. We waited for our companions. Denise returned to the security sector, but avoided our eyes and sat across the room. We waited for the two arguing aliens. I laid my head down on the desk.

The Enochian smell and the dead bodies on slabs in the morgue worked on my subconscious. I knew I was dreaming, but it seemed more of a memory.

Boudreau had called me into his Tripoli office, where he ran his part of the War. Lolich stood behind Boudreau's desk, sneering at me as I presented myself to the general. All three of us were dressed in desert fatigues.

He should have been court-martialed for cruelty to prisoners of war, I thought. My work was necessary. Experimentation on an alien biological system caused many deaths, which I did not relish, but more humans died in the battles . . . and we were losing. Lolich, on the other hand, tortured the Enochian prisoners for nothing more than to see them hurt. I figured that without the War and Boudreau's backing, Lolich would have been a serial killer. My dreaming self knew that I killed far more than Lolich.

"Captain, is Bio-Chem ready?"

I saw anger in his eyes. The Sahara Campaign had not been going well. "We've completed the trials," I said. "The mortality rate for Enochians is ninety-seven per-cent, with no residual effect on human populations. We have the agent we need. We also have the antidote for those Enochians who surrender."

"That's damn near ethnic cleansing," Boudreau said, ignoring my statement about an antidote. Lolich grinned and I understood why; there would be no sur-render allowed. Boudreau stared at me, but his mind was elsewhere. His eyes focused. "How long before it's useable?"

"The viral agent is being weaponized as we speak, General," I said. "We'll use drones to release it over their encampments."

"They'll shoot them down, I assume," Boudreau said.

I shrugged. "We're counting on it, sir. Even with their beam weapons, none of the virus will be de-stroyed. We've tested that repeatedly."

Boudreau said nothing. I waited for definitive word to release the agent. All we needed was the au-thorization. My eyes went to Lolich. He did not re-turn my stare, as he bent down and whispered into Boudreau's ear. Boudreau nodded and looked up.

"Proceed at your pace, Captain," he said.

"Yes, sir," I said, standing straighter. "Does that mean we have authorization to deploy the weapon, sir?"

Boudreau opened his mouth and closed it. He didn't want to give the order, it appeared. "Proceed at your pace," he said. "Dismissed."

I walked out of the office. He wanted deniability, that much was obvious, but the implication was clear. End this damn War.

The dream changed and I found myself wearing the protective suit worn by Chemical Warfare personnel. Sand pelted the plastic faceplate as the truck bounded through the desert. The virus had been released three days earlier, and one of the enemy camps had been secured. A small air conditioner moved air through the suit, but it did not cool the body enough in the hot, dry Saharan sun.

"Why do we have to wear these things?" I'd been in the field before, but not wearing the suit. "This virus will not infect humans."

"I'm sorry, sir," my driver, an innocuous corporal from the Chem-Bio unit, said. "The suit is not for the virus, sir. It's for the smell."

I opened my mouth. But all I was able to say was, "Oh."

We topped a dune and the Enochian outpost lay below us on the sandy floor. Activity appeared nonexistent as we rode closer, except for two human guards, dressed only in desert fatigues, standing post at the edge of the alien base. I understood what the corporal said. The smell permeated the chem suit and settled into my nostrils. Without the suit's filtering, the smell would be too much.

One of the guards held up a hand. "I need your authorization," he said.

"We're from Bio-Chem," my driver said as he handed our orders to the guard, who gave them a cursory inspection and handed them back.

"How can you stand the smell?" my driver asked.

The guard smiled and sucked in a deep breath. "Smells like victory to me," he said; then he laughed and shrugged. "You get used to it." He waved us through, slapping a half-hearted salute to me as we passed.

Bodies sprawled where they died. Black liquid surrounded most of them. I saw the characteristic boils of our version of the Black Death we'd unleashed upon the invaders. I turned over a body and saw that the hump on its back had blown open due to the pressure of the boils. I fought the urge to vomit; it would take too long to get out of the head gear.

Intelligence reports told us that the Enochian armies on Earth had ceased to be an effective fighting force. Ships had been seen jumping to orbit where their fleet stood by, waiting to land. I surveyed the death around me. If anyone in those ships had contracted the virus, then the fleet had a matter of days before sharing their army's fate.

Boudreau refused to allow me to release the antidote without a formal cessation of hostilities, but as I stood in the camp, I knew I had to do it, orders or not. Though I knew they'd killed my wife and that the Enochians had started this War, I could not let a species of sentient creatures all die because of my revenge.

Releasing the virus without his consent had not turned Boudreau against me and led to my court-martial.

Boudreau wanted the entire Enochian species eradicated from the universe. *Boudreau turned on me because I released the antidote.*

It had taken a dream and many years to realize why I was really court-martialed.

I awoke when my head was raised and dropped on the desk I had been leaning upon. Rising up, I rubbed my face and looked at Dingo, who stood over me, grinning in his Enochian-human fashion. I suggested a travel destination for him, but he shook his head.

"We don't have time and it's too damn hot, Captain," the alien said, his grin growing. "It's time to go back to New Orleans."

I blinked. "Did you get your new orders?"

His response surprised me. "Yes, it has been decided . . . you and I have been chosen as heroes." Dingo's smile faded. "As an Enochian, the only way you can be a hero is to be dead."

I gave a small, nervous laugh. "I have no intention of dying. And if you're going to be my partner, I expect you to assume the same attitude. Don't start getting fatalistic on me, Dingo."

Dingo stared at me as if I'd lost what little mind I had left. I smiled, and he puffed his jowls and walked away.

I got to my feet, unsteady from the catnap, and looked around. Gintomen and Martinez were waiting at the door as Dingo strode toward them. Denise was sitting across the room, staring into space. I walked over to her.

"Denise, I am truly sorry about Kristen," I said, bending down to talk into her ear. A tear ran down her face and I brushed it away and turned her face toward mine. "We will get her back."

She nodded. I caressed her face. She reached a hand up to mine and held it. She got up from the table, still holding my hand, and pulled me to her. She seemed to melt into my body. Only my wife had ever melted into me. I felt her warmth and her agony. We said nothing. After a few seconds, she pulled away and went to join the others. I followed.

Gintomen led the group toward the entrance of the building. The halls were as deserted as they had been when we first arrived. When we got to the door and stepped outside, I understood. Lining both sides of the sidewalk to Martinez's truck was the entire Enochian contingent from the administration building, with the notable exception of Rivera and her honor guards. Gintomen motioned for me to join him.

"Stimson, this parade is in your honor." The Enochian security chief gazed at me intently. "You may not realize the importance of your position amongst the Enochian Culture, but this is our way of showing our regard for you." Gintomen sounded awed.

Denise pulled my head toward her. "Enochians do not have parades, Roger," she whispered. "They're adapting a human custom to their culture in your honor. Walk slowly and stop at the body at the end of the steps."

I looked at the mutilated body of the rebel leader and nodded. Gintomen motioned for me to walk down the steps.

The assembled Enochians began to whistle and click as I descended the steps. I stopped when I reached the leader of the rebels and looked down at the body. I could see cuts and bruising on the naked alien. Pieces of flesh seemed to have been removed, as if taken as trophies of the encounter. My insides froze when I realized that the Enochian was still breathing. I stopped Denise as she was about to walk past me.

"He's still alive," I said urgently.

She nodded, but said nothing as she passed me, looking straight ahead toward the truck. Gintomen and Martinez passed me without stopping. Dingo was right behind them. When he reached me, Dingo stopped and looked around the crowd, which had become silent when the Enochian stopped beside me. Dingo glared down at the rebel leader, whose eyes opened and gazed blankly at Dingo and myself. I saw Dingo pull back his left leg and kick the wounded Enochian hard in the face. The crowd erupted in approval with clicks and whistles. Dingo walked on toward the truck.

For a moment, I was angry with Dingo for his cruel act, and then I realized that I thought of him in human terms. No matter how long Dingo had been among humans, he was full Enochian in thought, word, and deed. Dingo had done what Dingo should have done: relish the humiliation of an outcast, a rebel, a traitor.

I looked around the crowd, ignoring the dying alien at my feet. I could not help him, no matter what my nursing training told me to do. This was an Enochian custom. It was their way of vanquishing their foes, while sparing the followers.

The Enochians became silent. I nodded at both sides of the sidewalk and then my eyes caught sight of a golden tunic. Rivera stared down the steps. I glared back at the Enochian Rejected Prefect, but turned away without acknowledging her. I could hear a few angry clicks and whistles from the assembled crowd, but I was surprised at how few Enochians seemed angered by my rebuff of the local Prefect. I somehow felt that Rivera, and others who feared Earth, were responsible for this death and destruction, and for the assassination attempt. Though she had encouraged me to prevent another Human-Enochian War, I sensed that she would be more comfortable with humanity eliminated.

Rivera just did not want to be on the losing side of the Enochian uprising, I thought.

I got to the truck and climbed in without looking back, slamming the door behind me. Gintomen stood outside of my window. He seemed to be smiling. I nodded at the security chief. He nodded back and waved at Martinez to start driving.

Dingo laughed as we pulled away. "I take it you were not impressed by Rivera, Captain," Dingo said, still chuckling. "Gintomen noticed it and was impressed by you."

I ignored Dingo and kept my thoughts to myself. I watched with interest as we left the Enochian Reservation and headed back to Mescalero.

It was time to go home.

PART FOUR

NEW ORLEANS
AND
RAFTA

PROLOG

News report on the arrival of Enochian Prefect
to New Orleans, early Sunday morning.

The camera follows the descent of the Enochian ship. A reporter provides voiceover for the pictures.

Voice: We're picking up live pictures of the descent of the Enochian ship into the atmosphere of Earth. Sources have confirmed that the ship is carrying the Enochian Prefect to a summit meeting with President Gamble in New Orleans tomorrow morning.

The disc-shaped craft flies over the New Orleans skyline before descending to an open field in Uptown. The camera loses sight of the ship, so a recording of the descent begins running in a loop.

Voice: The White House press office has announced that a news conference will be held after the historic meeting. It has been hinted that the Enochian Prefect has come to Earth to formally end hostilities between the two species.

The picture cuts to a live shot of the disc on the ground in New Orleans.

Voice: We're going to stay with this shot and wait for what happens next. I have been informed that President Gamble's motorcade will be arriving in a few minutes for a formal welcome to the Enochian Prefect.

25

The flight back to New Orleans had been uneventful. Dingo, Denise, and I had showered and then slept for a couple of hours at the Martinez home before take-off. I caught a nap for much of the flight, this time uninterrupted sleep, no dreams. I awoke somewhere over Texas or Louisiana with a host of concerns and trepidations about the next day or so. Denise was awake, but in her own world. Dingo snored softly. I made no attempt to talk with either of my companions. We kept to ourselves, facing our own demons.

I imagined that Dingo's concerns rested on the Enochian soul. Many times, he had explained that our victory in the previous war had changed Enoch much more than it had changed Earth.

I knew that Denise had only one thing on her mind—the safety of her daughter.

I reflected on the trip to the Enochian Reservation. Dingo and Denise had manipulated me into making the trip, but I thought I understood why. The trip had little to do with information about Rafta, though I was certain that Dingo wanted as much intelligence as he could get. My visit to the Enochian Reservation had given me insight into Enochian intentions. It was one more way to entice me into helping them. I needed to know that the Enochians were enforcing their end of their secret bargaining with the governments of Earth. Thinking in terms of why they'd chosen the U.S. President as the Earth representative, I figured they went to the major military power on the planet. It was up to us to bring in the rest of humanity.

But what if there were bands of dissension among humans to the new treaty between humans and Enochians? I saw an image of the rebel leader at the bottom of the steps as I walked past him. Dingo's foot smashed into his face. Rivera's muted fear and disdain of humanity echoed in my mind. Would we have to ferret out the dissenters and subject them to the same indignity of the rebel leader? And how many of the Enochians were as reluctant to accept humans as the Prefect of the Rejected? I still called the Earthbound aliens "the Rejected," even though I knew they were actually a base camp for further Enochian military and intelligence-gathering activity on Earth.

I drifted back toward sleep, listening to the drone of the small airplane's engine, but this time dreams of exploding Earths, like Dingo's tattoo, made me sleep lightly and fitfully. I knew that Earth was at a cusp in the history of our species. The next twenty-four hours could see us make a leap for the stars. Or we could be totally obliterated by the Enochians. I jumped when the plane's alarm went off, banging my head on the low ceiling of the plane cabin.

"Captain, don't hurt yourself too bad," Dingo said, chuckling. "I am going to need your help tomorrow."

I gave him a look that left no doubt as to what destination I wished for him. I was tired, angry, and nervous as hell. Taking a deep breath and letting it out slowly, I calmed my emotions and gazed at Denise. She had not moved in the seat next to me.

"She didn't sleep at the Martinez's," Dingo said.

I nodded, absently. I could not understand how my feelings for her had deepened in such a short time. I wanted to protect her, provide for her, and keep her safe. I wanted to be her hero, her champion. *Damn, that sounds so sappy,* I thought. An image of her daughter filled my head. I looked at Denise, reached out, and caressed her face. *Right now, she needs a champion.* I hoped I could measure up to the task.

Denise's eyes opened and she smiled, but as soon as the smile formed, it vanished. She grabbed my hand, gave it a slight squeeze, and then dropped it as she sat up in the seat. "Are we in New Orleans?"

I nodded. She looked into my eyes and seemed to want to say something, but then she shook her head, almost imperceptibly, and turned to Dingo. "Have they made any other calls?"

"They have," Dingo replied. "While we slept, they've made three phone calls."

"Do we have any idea where they are?" Denise was anxious. She wanted her daughter back. "Can we find them?"

"We know what area of New Orleans they are in," Dingo said. "Now that we're here, we'll be able to pinpoint it down to the millimeter."

"While we're waiting, I think we need to pay a visit to James Williams," I said.

Denise nodded and sat back into her seat, closing her eyes again. No one spoke until we touched Louisiana soil.

Denise rapped on the door to James Williams's room. Dingo and I stood on either side of the door, out of view. Denise wouldn't spur the bodyguards to aggressive action in the way that Dingo and I would. I glanced around to make sure there were no cameras to give us away. If there were, they'd hidden them well. I saw the spyglass light go dark.

"What do you want?" I smiled as I recognized Ladner's

voice. I knew he would be happy to see me again. "Tell James that Denise Windham wants to see him," Denise said.

Ladner hesitated before responding. "What about?"

"Just tell him, damn it," she said. Her anger showed in her rigid posture and the scowl on her face.

I heard whispering on the other side of the door. I shook my head. These guys got paid for brawn, not smarts.

"Wait there," Ladner said. Heavy footsteps moved away, muffled by carpet. Denise glanced toward me and sighed. After a moment, I saw the spyglass darken again and more whispering followed. The door opened a crack.

Dingo opened it all the way with a kick, which sent Ladner flying across the room. As I rushed inside, I saw him lying on his back, apparently stunned. The other body-guard, Blake, stood a few feet away. I saw him reach into his jacket.

"Dingo!" As I yelled, Dingo jumped headfirst toward Blake. I heard the muffled pop of a .32. Dingo butted Blake in the chest. Blake flew toward the wall and dropped the gun when he hit.

Dingo rubbed the top of his head. "Damn, that hurts," he said. "And it pisses me off."

I had no time to answer. Ladner rolled to his knees and sprang to his feet, pulling his gun as he did so. I broke his wrist as I yanked the weapon from his hand. For good measure, I finished off the knee I'd kicked the other day.

"That'll be quite enough," Williams said. I looked up and saw him standing at the balcony door, a small-caliber pistol pointed in Dingo's direction. He glanced at me, but kept the gun on Dingo. "Ah, Captain Stimson, I knew I should have taken care of you when I had the chance."

Ladner moved and I kicked him in the face. He lost

consciousness. "I told you, Williams, that I'm not a captain anymore," I said. I pointed at the gun. "That little thing won't hurt my Enochian friend, at least not enough to keep him from killing you."

Williams frowned and cast a worried look toward me, then at Dingo.

"Just say the word, Captain," Dingo said. The Enochian stood ready to jump, glaring at Williams. I had no doubt that Williams would be dead before he decided to use the pistol. Dingo bared his teeth as he spoke. "Look at the top of my head, little human. See that bruise? That came from his gun." Dingo pointed at Blake, still out cold.

I figured Blake might live, if his aorta hadn't severed by the force of Dingo's head hitting his chest. Blake groaned and opened his eyes, staring at Dingo, his fear quite evident. The bodyguard had enough sense not to move.

"We're not here to kill you," I said. "We just have some questions."

Williams stared at me for a moment; then his eyes focused on something behind me. He laid the gun on a table beside the balcony door.

"Where's Kristen, James?" Denise walked up beside me, but she glared at Williams. "What the hell have you done with my daughter?"

Williams appeared confused. "What are you talking about?"

I had no patience for his dumb act. "Look you bastard, someone's kidnapped Kristen, trying to keep me away from Canal Street tomorrow morning," I said. I walked over to Williams and grabbed him by the throat and pushed him against the wall. "Where is the girl, Williams? You've got five seconds."

Williams's eyes bulged as much with fear as from the pressure I had on his throat. "I really don't know what you're talking about," he said, his voice raspy.

I slammed his head against the wall and watched him slide to the floor. I stepped toward him. He threw his hands in front of his face. "I really don't know," he said, whining. I hated whining. I reached down with the intention of squeezing his eyeballs out of his head, but I felt a soft touch on my forearm. Denise gave a quick shake of her head.

Williams looked up. Tears marked his cheeks and more began to flow. "Denise, whatever you may think of me, you have to know that I would never hurt Kristen." He looked at each of us and saw our disbelief. "It's true, I swear."

"Who took her, James?" I marveled at how calm Denise sounded.

He shook his head. "I don't know," he said. "I lost control of the Sons of Earth a long time ago. I get paid to be a figurehead."

I looked at Dingo. "Boudreau," I said. "He's running the Sons of Earth through this piece of crap." Dingo puffed. I decided the jowl puffing showed indifference and disgust.

"I didn't tell you that," Williams stammered. "If you want to know who took Kristen, look for that Lolich asshole."

Denise grabbed my arm and pulled me back a step. "I think he's telling the truth," she whispered.

Williams whimpered as he watched Dingo. "Yeah, me too," I said. "I really wanted to hurt him, but it wouldn't do any good. All I'd get is more guilt on my mind."

"I know," Denise said.

I leaned down and grabbed Williams's face. He tried to flinch away, but I held his jaw. "If I find out you're lying, Dingo and I will be back. You understand?"

Williams nodded.

I heard a buzz and saw Dingo reach into his pocket.

"They've called again," he said. "We've got their location narrowed down to a four-block section."

We filed out of the room. I stopped at the door.

"I think I'd hire better security, if I were you," I said. "Your best bet would be the New Orleans police, after the shit lands on Boudreau. You need to cut a deal early."

Williams put his head in his hands. I followed Dingo and Denise.

26

Two hours later, it was about four in the afternoon and we had been riding around a sixteen-square-mile area of warehouses and docks near the river. The kidnappers had not made a phone call since early afternoon. Dingo was convinced that we would know the exact location of the next call.

While we drove in circles, I thought about Williams. Someone—Boudreau probably, but I couldn't prove it—paid Williams to give speeches and stay in ritzy hotels as a front for something much more sinister than the public persona of the Sons of Earth. His organization had turned into a clandestine terror cell, with the Enochians as their target. I realized that the new Sons of Earth would have no qualms about using an Enochian assassin against President Gamble and the Enochian Prefect.

Dingo's laptop beeped, interrupting my thoughts. He pulled over to the side of the road and began furiously punching keys. We didn't speak. I could see the fear and apprehension on Denise's face. After a couple of moments of intense activity, Dingo yelled, "Got the slimy bastards."

He turned the computer screen toward us. A bright red dot glowed on the map, three blocks from the green dot that indicated our location on the area map. I looked at Denise, who had closed her eyes and had begun to breathe deep, even breaths. I cut my eyes toward Dingo.

"Let's go get Kristen," I said. Dingo let out an Enochian war cry, which sounded a lot like a cat whose tail was just trampled by an errant foot. We lurched forward as Dingo slapped the truck into gear.

We parked about a block away from the building they had made the call from, discussing our options. Reason and a bit of fear had tempered my earlier reaction.

"We really need to call the police and let them handle this situation," I said. It was the right thing to do, whether I liked it or not. I looked at the target building, knowing that Lolich should be somewhere near.

Dingo disagreed. "Captain, if we call the police, then you and I are likely to spend the next couple of days in jail before they sort all this out. That would be too late to stop the assassination attempt." Dingo puffed hard and turned to Denise. "But she is your daughter. I'll do this whatever way you wish."

Denise nodded, but said nothing.

I felt helpless to help her. "We don't know what we are facing."

"I can solve that," Dingo said, opening the door to the truck. "You guys stay here. If I'm not back in twenty minutes, call the police if you decide."

Before I could protest, he slammed the door and ran toward the corner of the building in front of us.

"Damn alien," I said. "Does he know what the hell he's doing?" I could see him as he reached the corner. I turned to Denise. "Look, if we're not back in ten minutes, call the New Orleans police." She nodded. I got out and ran for the corner to join Dingo.

The air was cool for a late January afternoon, but I did not feel the cold. Adrenaline pumped through my veins, warming me as I ran. I reached the corner.

"Glad you could join me, Captain," Dingo said, wearing a stupid grin.

I glanced at the Enochian from head to toe. At least he had changed back into human clothes and out of that white tunic. I grinned back. "I couldn't let a damn fool Enochian run into the streets of New Orleans all alone. The last time you were alone here, you ended up in my emergency room."

He puffed, dismissing my comments. "Let's go."

Dingo took off toward the back of the warehouse. I hoped there wouldn't be a guard posted there. We reached the back door. He had trotted to allow me to stay up with him and to save his strength. I put my hand on the back doorknob. Dingo knocked my hand away. I glared, about to complain, but he pointed at a yellow wire running along the top of the door. Either an alarm or a booby-trap. Remembering my apartment, I figured the door was wired with explosives. These guys liked firecrackers, usually big and destructive, if the holes in my apartment gave any indication as to their predilections. Dingo motioned for me to follow him.

Along the side of the four-story building was a set of fire escapes that came down to the second-floor level, a good fourteen feet above my head. I gaped up and then looked at Dingo. "I can't make the jump up there."

He puffed at me. "Remember the Riverwalk, Captain," he said, as he grabbed me along the waist and jumped to catch the rail of the metal steps.

I expected to hear the rusting metal groan and then collapse under our combined weight, but the stairs held and I climbed over the railing. I saw an open window on the third floor and pointed it out to Dingo. We crept up the fire escape, glancing in windows, trying to spot anything of the kidnappers or Kristen. The old metal creaked with our steps and I feared we would give ourselves away. On the third floor, Dingo motioned for me to go in first.

Light filtered into the empty room from behind. I smelled the musk of disuse and rat droppings as I let my eyes adjust to the light. Dingo slid through the window and crouched beside me. I thought I could hear muffled talking coming from my right. I patted the alien on the leg and moved off, not checking to see if the Enochian followed me.

The door stood slightly ajar and I saw a dim light emanating from beyond it. I stuck my head up to the crack. The voices were still muffled, but I thought I could hear them coming from below. The floor outside of the room turned into a kind of metal catwalk, which ringed a larger opening below. I opened the door to slink out onto the catwalk. The door squeaked. The talking below me stopped. I froze.

I could hear footsteps getting louder as they came toward me. They stopped almost directly below. I held my breath. I think Dingo did, too.

I heard a rustling to my left, but I didn't dare turn to look. A clicking noise came from below and then an explosion deafened my ears. I waited for the burning pain of a gunshot wound. But I felt nothing. Scurrying little feet came toward me fast. A rat appeared in the opened door. I buried my face and felt its claws scramble over me to get to safety.

"Damn rat," the male voice from below said. "I hate those things."

"What the hell do you think you're doing?" another voice screamed, muffled somewhat from distance and the buffers of walls. I heard the anger in the second man's voice. "We don't need the cops out here."

"Relax," said the man I named Rat Hater, his voice becoming fainter as he walked away from me toward the other voice. "There ain't nobody out here on Sundays. That's why I picked this place."

I let out a ragged sigh, realizing that my jaw hurt from the momentary tension. I shook for a few seconds and thought, *Now, why in hell am I here, instead of the police?* I turned around to whisper the question to Dingo. He wasn't there.

"Great," I muttered, softly. "Now what?"

I sat there, wondering where the alien had gone. I took a deep breath and let it out, calming myself further. I decided to check out the situation, which was the reason I followed Dingo into this building.

I noticed that part of the metal walkway stayed in the shadow, so I figured if I stayed close to the wall, I could move without being seen by the Rat Hater and his angry friend. As slowly and quietly as I could, I stood up and slid into the shadow, just outside the door. The smell of mold joined the mustiness, creating a smell that would only be challenged by an unbathed Dingo. Looking around, I noticed that the catwalk surrounded an open area about ten feet below me. From this position, I could not see the men with the guns, but I heard them talking. I moved toward the muffled voices. The catwalk took a ninety-degree turn and, though I was still hidden in the darkness, below me the floor opened up into a large area well lit by a floodlight.

I saw two men sitting at a card table. Two nasty-looking automatic weapons lay on the table in front of them. Kristen sat on a mattress along the only wall. She was tied at the wrists, and that rope was fastened to a chain that encircled a column. The girl looked dirty and unkempt, but otherwise healthy. I wanted to keep her that way. I took another step toward the alcove, when I felt something hit my stomach hard. I bent over and let out a grunt as I fell to my knees into the light. The two men at the table scrambled to their feet, grabbing their weapons and aiming them toward me.

"What the hell?" A voice below me couldn't seem to believe what he was seeing.

I heard the clicking of a gun and felt something cold and hard against the back of my neck.

"Don't move," said the man behind me. I did not move. He spoke to the people below. "I am so damn glad that you two are in charge of this operation." His voice was calm and detached, with a hint of danger toward the two men below us. I had heard the voice before, but couldn't place it, being too busy trying to return to normal breathing. The two men relaxed somewhat, though I sensed they feared the man who had captured me.

"Get up, Stimson, slowly," he said, accentuating the directions with a small upward movement of the gun barrel against my neck. "Do not doubt that I will kill you." I did not doubt him at all. I said nothing. I recognized the voice and the demeanor.

He guided me toward a set of metal stairs, gun still on the back of my neck. We descended together. We walked toward the table. As we got there, a hand grabbed my shoulder and flung me toward the wall on the opposite side of the table from Kristen. I picked my face off the cold, concrete floor and glared at my captor.

It was Lolich, Boudreau's bodyguard.

27

"Watch him," Lolich said. One of the men came within five feet of me, leveling a gun in my direction. The man's attention was still on Lolich, who took a deep breath and let it out hard, as if frustrated. "Who the hell did the shooting and why?"

"We heard a noise," one of the men said, his voice quivering. I realized I was right; he was afraid of Lolich. He should have been. I knew the horrors of which Lolich was capable. "I saw a rat and I shot at it. I hate those damn things." Rat Hater stood up straight to show that he wasn't afraid. I could see his legs wobbling as he stood defiant.

Lolich saw it, too. He smiled. Returning his weapon to its shoulder holster, Lolich walked up to Rat Hater, still smiling. I saw the blur of a right hand flash from Lolich's side as he backhanded the other man. The one guarding me flinched at the sound of Lolich's hand impacting on Rat Hater's face. Rat Hater was on the ground, moaning. Lolich reached down, grabbed the man by his shirt, and pulled him to his feet.

Still smiling, Lolich brushed off Rat Hater's clothes and said in a low, menacing voice, "Don't ever disobey my orders, again." The man shook his head and Lolich released him.

His orders, I thought. *Then, Boudreau is not only involved in this thing, he probably planned the entire operation.*

I sat doubled over on the floor with a look of pain on my face. My abdomen still hurt, but the pain had subsided enough that I could move. I just didn't want Lolich to know that. I was catching my breath, watching for an opportunity to overpower my guard and get his automatic rifle. Lolich had to be taken alive to prove Boudreau's involvement in this affair. However, capturing Lolich was going to be tough, if not damn near impossible, since he had nothing to lose in a fight against me. I knew that he was most probably going to kill us. I had to wait for my chance and hope that Dingo would give it to me. *And just where the hell is Dingo?* I thought.

Lolich walked toward me. "Well, Stimson, we meet again so soon," he said, grinning. "Why am I not surprised? You should have joined us when the senator asked you to."

I saw a blur of movement in my direction. I reacted, catching his hand before it struck my face.

Lolich laughed. "I see you kept your skills up," he said. The smile left his face. "Unfortunately, we don't have time for competition. As you can see, I am busy at the moment."

He turned away from me. I wanted to jump to my feet and break his back with one kick, but I realized I would die before he did.

Lolich walked away. "Stay away from his hands and feet," he said, talking to my guard. "If he moves, kill him, because he will surely kill you." My guard's eyes widened, and he took a couple of steps back.

Lolich walked to Kristen and stopped, standing over her, smiling. He reached down and stroked her hair. The girl retreated from his touch.

"Leave me alone," she said, fear softening her voice. I could tell that she was tired. She looked up at Lolich, pleading. "Let me go home."

Lolich shook his head. "Can't do that, princess. Want to know why?" Kristen said nothing and hung her head.

Lolich spoke as if she had answered. "Okay, I'll tell you. You can't go home right now, because your mother is a bigger fool than we thought she was." He pointed his thumb toward me over his shoulder.

"She sent this guy and a damn Enochian to try to rescue you," he said as he turned toward me. "Stimson, here, was stupid enough to get caught, and now he can link my boss with your kidnapping and our plans for tomorrow." He turned back to Kristen, continuing to talk loud enough to make sure that I heard.

"And Stimson is probably the one person who could convince the aliens and our government that Boudreau was the one really behind this fiasco, which means that all of you have to be eliminated." Lolich watched the girl for a reaction.

"What do you mean by 'eliminated'?" Kristen asked. She was too young to understand that she could die.

Lolich reached out a hand as if to caress her face. Kristen pulled away, but he caught a handful of her hair. She screamed as he pulled her face close to his.

"It means that I am going to have to kill Stimson, the alien Dingo, your mother, and—" he brought her face right up to his "—I'm going to have to kill you." With those words, he threw her back down to the concrete floor beside the mattress they had provided for her. I could see her shoulders convulsing with sobs.

"You're a sadistic son of a bitch, Lolich," I said in a quiet voice. I could feel the anger trying to burst through the surface of my carefully checked emotions. Anger would only inhibit my ability to do what I needed to do in the next few minutes. Lolich ignored me.

"I'm going to kill you, Lolich," I said withholding my anger. Lolich laughed and told my guard to shut me up, but before he had the opportunity, all hell broke loose.

Rat Hater had been posing with his assault rifle balanced on his hip and pointed in the air. It was a practiced pose for which I'm sure he stood for hours before a mirror. He had that fake "I am a badass" look on his face. He had watched the interactions of Lolich with Kristen and me when he should have been protecting their perimeter. Hadn't he heard Lolich say that an Enochian was still loose in the building? Again, as with Williams's bodyguards, men had been picked for other qualities than brains. I heard a loud yell from his direction and looked up to see a rat, which happened to look a lot like the one we had all encountered earlier, on the Rat Hater's shoulders. The rat appeared to be gnawing on Rat Hater's ear.

My guard turned toward his compatriot and stared in disbelief. I jumped to my feet and broke his kneecap from the side. I grabbed his rifle as he hit the ground, screaming in pain. I saw Lolich move out of the corner of my eye, but another movement caught my attention. A blue blur dropped from the catwalk and onto Rat Hater and the squealing rodent. In a few seconds, Dingo was holding the assault rifle, and Rat Hater's neck was at an extremely odd angle to the rest of his body, a condition that was not conducive for life. The rat scrambled away unharmed and disappeared into the shadows.

"Put the rifles down!" I turned toward Lolich's voice. He was holding a pistol next to Kristen's midsection, with the girl shielding him from Dingo and myself. "I'll kill her, Stimson, and you know it. You and that damned alien should put down your weapons."

I looked at Dingo, who was glaring at Lolich. "Put it down, Dingo," I said. The alien's grip tightened around the rifle momentarily. But then he tossed the gun toward Lolich's feet. I did the same thing.

"I'm sorry, princess," Lolich said to Kristen, "but this is where we all part company." He looked up. "You should have been helping us, Stimson. Too bad, though."

"Put the gun down!" a Cajun-accented voice shouted from behind Lolich. Lolich tightened his grip on Kristen, but otherwise did not move. "Put it down and let the girl go." Something was oddly familiar about the voice, but I was a bit too stressed to know what at the time. I saw movement from the shadows behind Lolich. A small, rather rotund man stepped into the light.

"Devereaux?" I couldn't believe my eyes. I didn't say anything else.

Lolich hadn't moved. "Put your gun down, or I'll kill the girl."

Devereaux did not respond.

"I'll kill her, damn it." No response. Lolich swung around fast, still using Kristen as a shield. Now he had his back against the wall and could see Devereaux, Dingo, and myself.

"I'm going to walk out of here with the girl and you're going to let me," Lolich said. He was getting nervous, which meant that the danger to all of us, especially to Kristen, had increased.

Devereaux shook his head. "Not gonna happen," the detective said.

"I'll kill her." Lolich was shrill.

I heard Denise's voice in the distance. "Kristen," she yelled.

"Momma," Kristen answered and began to struggle with Lolich.

I started to yell at her not to move, when I heard the gunshot. Kristen looked surprised and then slumped over in Lolich's arms. I saw blood appear on her shirt as she yelled in agony. Lolich's mouth opened in shock and then the back of his head exploded. Blood and brain tissue splattered the wall behind him. He let go of Kristen, fell back against the wall, and slid to the floor.

I ran to Kristen. Sucking sounds were escaping from the holes in her chest, in the side and in the front. I knew that one of her lungs had collapsed.

"Get away from the girl," an unfamiliar voice barked at me. I ignored the order and applied pressure to the wounds. "I said, back away from the girl."

"Go to hell," I said, harshly. "Get an ambulance on the way, stat." I didn't look around when I heard the cocking of a gun. "That means now, damn it."

"Leave him alone," Devereaux said to the other cop. "He's a nurse. Now do as he said and get the paramedics in here." I heard footsteps disappearing in the distance. I kept my attention on Kristen and her wounds.

"Hold on, Kristen. You're going to be all right." I hoped that my voice was convincing. Kristen nodded. Her screaming had stopped, but she was beginning to struggle for air due to the collapsed lung. I felt another body beside me. Denise. "We're going to get her to the emergency room and get her treated."

Tears streamed down Denise's face, but her voice sounded calm. "How serious is this?"

I looked her in the eyes. "She has two bullet holes in her right lung, which means that air and, more than likely, blood are keeping her from being able to breathe," I said. "Denise, this is a very serious injury, but I have seen people live through worse."

The paramedics arrived on the scene. I demanded a petrolatum gauze dressing from them and taped it on three sides to both wounds. An emergency medical technician put a nonrebreather oxygen mask on her and told me they were transporting her to the nearest hospital—Memorial Hospital, where I worked. I let the paramedics have her and turned to Denise.

"Go with them," I said. "Dingo and I will be there as soon as we can."

She grabbed my neck and kissed me lightly on the lips. I felt butterflies in my stomach. "Thank you, Roger."

I nodded and watched her leave at a trot to keep up with the stretcher. I sat down against the wall about three feet from where Lolich lay, staring into nothingness. I'm sure I had probably leaned against his blood, but I was too tired to care and too worried about Kristen. I felt a bit sorry that I had not killed him myself but, on the other hand, I was disappointed that Boudreau's bodyguard had died. Without testimony from this now-dead piece of crap, I couldn't reasonably link Boudreau to the plot against the Enochian Prefect and President Gamble. No one would take James Williams's word over that of a United States Senator. I sighed.

"Been busy, eh Captain?"

I looked up and stared at Devereaux hard. "You're supposed to be dead. And I'm the one who supposedly killed you."

Devereaux nodded at me. "Sorry about that. A necessary fiction, for certain, Stimson. At least you don't have to explain to my eighty-year-old father that his son is not dead. He believes everything he sees on the news channels." He changed the subject. "Will the girl be all right?"

"I think so, but her wounds are critical. And I'm not sure if anything major was hit, except for her lung. It'll be a long night for Denise." I closed my eyes.

Devereaux stood in silence for a few moments and then kicked my foot. "Come on, let's collect that damn blue friend of yours and go to the hospital. I'll fill you in on the way."

Dingo was surrounded by uniformed New Orleans police officers, all of whom had their service revolvers pulled and aimed at him. All they knew was that they were searching for an Enochian. They knew that all Enochians were blue and that there weren't very many of them—two to be precise, but they only knew about one—in New Orleans. Dingo was the obvious candidate to be the Enochian for whom they searched.

Dingo appeared harried when he caught Devereaux's eye. "Detective, will you get these people away from me? Tell them I'm not the blue alien they're looking for."

Devereaux laughed. "He's not the blue alien you're looking for," he said, chuckling. "Put your guns away." A few of the officers hesitated. "Back off, now!" Devereaux yelled. The officers complied, but didn't seem very happy.

"Thank you, Detective," Dingo said, as he eyed the officers who still watched him. "We have work to do, Captain."

"It'll wait," I said. "I need to check on Kristen and Denise."

On the way to the hospital, Devereaux said the shootout in the morgue convinced him that there was something to Dingo's story. He tried talking to the Secret Service, but Michele Allen told him that they had the security of the President well in hand. As for the security of the Enochian Prefect, well, they wanted to know where Devereaux had gotten his information, but were otherwise unconcerned.

The entire conversation pissed Devereaux off something fierce. He went to his captain and told him the entire story. His captain gave him permission to become the NOPD's freelance investigator for the state visit by the alien Prefect, but since he had been in a shootout with one of the possible participants of the assassination attempt, Devereaux decided he had better do things from behind the scenes. He confirmed Dingo's story of Rafta and the subsequent events surrounding our recent stay in New Mexico. Sheriff Martinez had informed him of the kidnapping of Kristen Windham and that we had a way of finding the kidnappers.

"We had the building staked out when you two went inside," he said. "When we saw the other man enter, we decided we had to act."

"You don't know who Lolich was, do you?" I was incredulous.

Devereaux raised an eyebrow. "Should I?"

"Denny Lolich was the personal bodyguard of Louisiana Senator Rafe Boudreau." Devereaux's mouth fell open, and then he closed it to whistle. "Boudreau's involved, Detective, but I can't prove it."

"That explains why my captain told me that I was dead until this thing was solved. He also told me that if I didn't solve the thing, I just might end up dead for real." Devereaux blinked once and then looked at me. "I thought he was kidding, but he wasn't."

"No," I said, shaking my head. "He wasn't kidding. Hell, they've been trying to kill Dingo and me. What made you think they wouldn't have tried to kill you?"

"Remember the morgue, Stimson," Devereaux said. "They did try to kill me. I just don't die that easily, thank God." He crossed himself and grinned at me. "It's pretty obvious you don't, either."

We pulled into the Memorial parking lot before I could respond.

I got out of Dingo's truck with Devereaux. Dingo had

been quiet throughout the ride to the ER, but he spoke to me through the lowered window. "Tell Denise that I wish for the best, Captain, but I have preparations to make for tomorrow." He hesitated and looked at Devereaux. "That is, if you are through with me, Detective Devereaux."

Devereaux nodded. "One of the only things I learned from the U.S. Secret Service was that I was to leave you alone, sir," he said. "They didn't tell me why."

Dingo nodded. "Take a cab to my house, Captain. You and Denise are welcome there as long as you need a place to stay."

I thanked the alien and watched him drive off, then turned and walked through the automatic doors with Devereaux behind me.

Kristen's condition was listed as critical and Bill Hubbard, the ER attending physician, said she was being prepped for immediate surgery to repair the holes and check for damaged blood vessels. I walked into the trauma room. Denise stood by the stretcher.

My eyes were drawn to the patched hole in the wall beside the door, where Dingo had impaled his head three days before. Hesitating, I remembered Larry, the two paramedics, Dr. Richards, and Shirley, who had saved my life by calling me just before Rafta murdered her and her husband.

I looked at Kristen. A tube protruded from her chest, attached to suction by way of a closed chest drainage system. I noticed the large amount of blood in the collection bucket of the suction on the wall.

Denise spoke without looking up. "She may not live through the surgery." Her eyes were red and swollen from crying. "She's lost a lot of blood."

I put my hand on her shoulder and squeezed. "Kristen is in the best hands possible." I looked at the girl on the stretcher. A breathing machine pumped air into her lungs on a steady basis. A unit of blood was transfusing into an IV. Her blood pressure was stable. "I'm sorry she got pulled into this mess, Denise. I am truly sorry."

I wondered if I could have done something different back at the warehouse. Part of me wished I had killed Lolich while I had the chance. I felt Denise's shoulder heave under my hand. I put my arms around her. She melted into me, crying.

"Ma'am?" I glanced up to see one of the OR nurses standing in the door. "We're ready to take her up to surgery." I steadied Denise as she leaned over her daughter and kissed her on the cheek, whispering encouragement into her ear. We left the room.

Denise turned to me. "Roger, I'm sorry that I got you involved in this," she said, tears still streaming down her face. "It was my idea to bring you into the investigation. I'm sorry."

I hugged her. "Don't be sorry." I pulled away from her and gazed into her eyes, stroking her hair lightly. "And you forget about anything else but Kristen."

"I can't think of anything else," she replied as she watched Kristen being readied to be wheeled away. "But you have to succeed tomorrow for Kristen's future. She's going to live, damn it. She has to." The operating room team pulled the stretcher out of the room.

I handed her a telephone number. "After I leave here, I'll be at Dingo's house. Call us and let us know how she's doing, please." She nodded absently, watching the stretcher roll down the hall. "Go be with your daughter." She gave me a small smile and followed the stretcher.

Two uniformed police officers filed past me, following her. I turned around and saw Devereaux leaning against the nurse's station. I ignored him as I walked over to the ward clerk and told her to page the nursing supervisor. She called back within minutes, and after I explained the situation to her, she said a room would be provided for Denise just outside the intensive care unit. I turned to Devereaux.

"How long have you known that woman?"

"Three days," I responded.

"I talked to her while you were finding out about the girl's condition," Devereaux said. "I'm impressed." He narrowed his eyes. "She's been pretty impressed with you, too, Stimson." I didn't say anything. Devereaux shrugged and changed the subject.

"The only kidnapper left alive is ready to spill his guts," Devereaux said; then he broke into a humorless grin. "Well, he will be when I get through with him. Seems that he didn't sign on for a couple or three murder charges. Want to come watch me do my job?"

"No, I think I'd better go to Dingo's and see what he has planned for tomorrow. She's going to be in room two-fifteen. Can you place a guard outside her room?"

"Way ahead of you," Devereaux said. "Both Mrs. Windham and the girl will have protection through the night."

Devereaux had one of his officers drive me to Dingo's house. The alien was not home, but the front door had been left unlocked. I fell down on the couch in the sitting room and fell asleep with the thought that maybe all of this would be over after tomorrow.

28

After cold, windy days for the last week, the sun warmed to the low seventies for the parade, proving that cold days do not linger in New Orleans, even in January. I scanned the crowd in front of the reviewing stand. Behind me, President Gamble and the Enochian Prefect sat watching one of the parades. I don't remember which Crewe hosted this event, but it didn't matter. The Prefect seemed to find humans clamoring for plastic beads and other baubles worth only pennies quite amusing.

I was somewhat surprised to find Senator Rafe Boudreau with the assembly of dignitaries. He smiled and nodded. I tried to look disgusted and ignored him. His appearance at this function was a message to me that no one could prove his involvement in any conspiracy, much less in an attempt on the life of President Gamble. And I had better not bring it up. Unfortunately, James Williams had disappeared soon after our visit to his hotel room, so my best witness as to Boudreau's involvement had apparently left for a safer haven. Williams knew the situation in New Orleans was about to explode.

Devereaux had called this morning and told me that the guard at the warehouse had refused to speak to police, but had yet to ask for a lawyer, so there was hope. He was a low-echelon member of the Sons of Earth. I doubted the man could implicate Boudreau, even though he was taking orders from Lolich. The Secret Service agent in charge of security for this summit between two species, Michele

TERRY BRAMLETT

Allen, told Devereaux that if there had ever been a threat to Gamble and the Enochian Prefect, then we ended that threat by killing and capturing the kidnappers last night.

"What does she think about Rafta?" I had asked the question, knowing that the rogue Enochian had not been found despite Devereaux's and the New Orleans Police Department's mammoth efforts.

"She thinks Rafta is a manifestation of the guilt you have over your actions during the War," he'd said before the parade started. "She doesn't like the fact that you are here."

I shook my head and grimaced. "Why the hell not?"

"Allen thinks you're an unstable personality who might try to harm the Enochian Prefect," Devereaux said. He chuckled. "If I were you, Stimson, I wouldn't move too close to President Gamble. Allen just might shoot you."

I shook my head again, remembering the conversation.

I glanced toward the stage, which was almost completely surrounded by bulletproof material. The only way an individual could get to the stand was to come in from the side. Secret Service agents were everywhere, studying the crowd. Allen glanced in my direction, but otherwise had ignored me all day. I was far from devastated. I wondered if my involvement was really required, but Dingo had insisted this morning that the Enochians expected me to be present. That damned "formidable enemy" legend they have, which is probably the reason Allen tolerated my presence. I was sure that I was being watched. I shrugged at the thought and observed the crowd as the floats went past, but my mind drifted to last night and a phone call from Denise.

Dingo had just given me the pass I would need to get through security and was ranting about the fact that the Secret Service said that the Enochian security contingent—

Dingo, myself, and two bodyguards from the Enochian Prefect's Honor Guard—were not allowed to carry weapons. He angrily stated that the Secret Service was determined to make him become a hero on Enoch, which meant that he would have to have died in the actions for his people. Dingo was not ready to die. I let him vent his frustrations. Personally, I did not wish to have a weapon in a public venue that would be as crowded as Canal Street was going to be on Monday.

Dingo answered the phone the moment it rang. "Yes?" He waited for a response and then started talking real fast, his excitement evident with the speed of his words. "Denise, how is Kristen? Is she going to be all right? What? Oh, okay." He turned to me, listening to Denise, but whispering to me, "She told me to shut up so she could talk. That's great, Denise," he said, still looking at me. "Yeah, he wants to talk." Dingo handed me the phone and left the room.

I hesitated for a moment before I brought the phone to my ear. "Tell me about Kristen," I said. I was concerned about her and felt like I should have stayed with her during the surgery, but I had gotten the impression that Denise had wanted to be alone.

"She came through the surgery fine, Roger," Denise answered. She sounded tired and emotionally drained. "She's in Intensive Care right now, but the doctor said she'll be going to a regular room by this Thursday, if there are no complications."

"That's great, Denise." I breathed a sigh of relief. "She should be out of the hospital in a week or two. What did he say about rehab?" *Are you going to be staying in New Orleans?* I could not ask her that question. She knew.

"They told me Kristen should be able to go home in a

couple of weeks, if she continues to improve," she said, and hesitated. "The doctor is going to set up her rehabilitation treatments in Midland before we leave."

There it was. Denise had completed her mission and almost gotten her daughter killed because of it. I would be a reminder of her mistakes and of her bad decisions that had endangered Kristen. I was silent on the phone, and so was she for a few seconds.

"Roger, I manipulated you into the position you're in," she said. I was silent. My stomach tried to reject her words, even though I already knew the truth. Denise pulled the master puppeteer strings to which I had danced for the last few days. "I set the whole thing in motion to get you involved."

"How did you do that?" I thought I hid my emotion from my voice. "Did you get Rafta to throw that grenade into my apartment or kill all of those people?"

"No, of course not," she said, and her voice fell to a whisper. "But I did let it be known that you were involved in the Enochian security effort. And I sent Dingo to see you. I didn't realize that they would try to eliminate everyone who came into contact with him."

I kept my silence. I wanted to know what her real feelings were for me, but I did not ask.

"I was contacted by Gintomen about the plot and asked if I would be prepared to help them," she said. "I agreed and, a couple of days later, Dingo called me with a plan." She sighed and appeared to wait for my reaction to her full confession. Denise had no more reason to lie or mislead me, so I decided that the full truth was coming out. I stayed silent, waiting for her to finish.

"The summit was going to be held in New Orleans, mainly due to the fact that you were living there," she said.

"You really don't understand the 'formidable enemy' concept the Enochians have. I admit, neither do I, but it was vital to them that you be involved in the summit meeting. But then they found out about the assassination attempt. They wanted your help."

I couldn't hold my silence any longer. "Why the hell didn't they just ask me?" I could hear irritation dripping from the words. I was upset and angry. I had known that I was being led around by a string, but even now I didn't want to believe that she had been the puppet master. I don't know how long I had known, but I still didn't want to hear her confession.

"They were afraid that you would say no, Roger," she said. I knew that she had heard my anger. "I am responsible for the deaths of your coworkers and the injuries to my own daughter, but I had to do it." She choked back sobs.

"I was wrong in my book, when I said that the virus was not needed to end the War. The Enochians had invaded our planet, and we weren't going to negotiate with them until they had been driven off Earth. They had made the decision to wipe out the entire human population, but the release of the virus stopped them in their tracks. I knew that you didn't know all that."

"Denise, you're not responsible for the things that Rafta did," I said, my anger somewhat dulled by the pain and emotion she showed in her admission to me. "You couldn't have known."

"Shut up and let me finish!" I was shocked by her vehemence. I shut up. "Roger, I played on the guilt that I knew you felt over the decision to release the virus, though I knew the truth. I knew you were infatuated with me from the moment we met, and I used that against you too."

I knew all that. I had known almost from the start, but it

still hurt, hearing it from her.

"I am very sorry, Roger. I truly am." We were both quiet for a moment.

"You were just doing what you thought was right," I said. "I understand why you helped the Enochians. I would have probably done the same thing." My reaction surprised me. Even though this woman had not been truthful with me and had manipulated my life over the last few days, I truly understood that she had no choice. My crush was as strong as it had ever been.

She didn't say anything, so I continued. "As for my emotions, my feelings for you," I said in a stammering voice, "well, I'm a thirty-eight-year-old man. I shouldn't be acting like a schoolboy."

"That's just it. Though I used your feelings for me against you, I came to realize that you were an honorable man, not the madman that the media had depicted. I began to regret that I was using you." I heard her voice catching, as if she were speaking through tears. "I wish we could have met under different circumstances. I need some time to think about this, to separate my feelings from the adrenaline. You do, too."

Part of me brightened at hearing her words, but all I said was, "Yeah. You're probably right." The phone was quiet for a long time, except that I thought I heard her crying.

"James called last night," she said. "He reiterated that he didn't have anything to do with the kidnapping. He was in the dark."

"What did you expect him to say, Denise? Did you think he would have confessed that he engineered the whole thing?"

"Roger, he was scared," she whispered. "He said that he knew who had done it and would take care of the matter. I think he's going to turn against the senator."

My eyebrows shot up. "Did he mention Boudreau by name?"

"No, but if the police put pressure on James, he'll crack. I know him. He's not that strong. He just likes the power and attention he gets."

"I'll mention it to Devereaux," I said. "They'll have to find him first. Williams went missing after our visit. According to the hotel staff, he didn't take the time to check out of his room."

The line fell silent again. After a few seconds, she said she would call before they left and hung up the phone. I held the receiver for a long time afterward.

Something wet dripped onto my shirt. I didn't realize that I had been crying. Tears had welled up in my eyes as I gazed at the parade, remembering the phone call. I turned and glared at Boudreau, who was laughing and pointing at the crowd, the epitome of a southern senator. "Your ass is going to fall, Boudreau," I mumbled to myself.

An odor drifted into my nostrils from the crowd. I turned around and saw the Prefect sitting in his seat, his two guards on either side. On the other end of the platform, Dingo stood, glaring into the crowd. All of the Enochians were accounted for. I knew that Rafta was in the crowd in front of me. I saw a figure moving toward the review stand, pushing people out of his way.

I went to meet him.

29

"He's got a gun," I heard somebody yell. People screamed and moved out of Rafta's way. The alien pulled off the cloak he was wearing to reveal a warrior's gold tunic without the associated body armor. Rafta was clothed in the manner of an ancient Enochian warrior, but the weapon he carried was anything but ancient.

As I ran toward him, I saw two Secret Service agents move to cut the alien off, putting themselves between Rafta and the bulletproof encasement surrounding the stand. Without looking, I knew that the Enochian guards had stepped in front of the Prefect to give their lives for their leader, in the same way that Secret Service agents were shielding President Gamble. I couldn't see them, but I assumed the agents began trying to clear the stand and get the President and the Prefect to safety.

One of the agents between Rafta and the reviewing stand fired his revolver, and the alien staggered back a step, then pointed his weapon at the shooter. A flash of light and the agent was gone. Only a scorch mark remained against the stage. The bulletproof glass around the stand simply melted with the intense heat. The other agent fired and Rafta burned him to oblivion. I ran hard toward Rafta.

I know the alien heard me and saw me, but I don't think he thought I would reach him before he got to the stage. I wasn't a threat to him in his mind, so he did not take the time to shoot me. I saw him bend his legs to jump. As Rafta left the ground, I hit him broadside in the air.

We landed on the stage, the alien landing on top of my left arm. I felt an intense pain and screamed as Rafta rolled off me and retrieved his weapon, which had fallen a few feet to his left. He picked up the weapon and aimed toward the Prefect. I saw the flash of light and knew that the beam would cut through the guards and the Prefect, burning anything in its path. I hoped they had time to evacuate before Rafta fired.

I jumped to my feet, ignoring the excruciating pain in my left arm. I jumped at Rafta feet first, catching the alien in the midsection and dislodging his weapon from his hands. It flew off the stage. I glanced toward the area where the Prefect and the President were sitting only seconds before, but neither of the leaders was visible. I saw one of the Enochian guards down on the stage. Another Enochian lay near him, not moving. I jumped to my feet, my left arm dangling uselessly from my side. It was broken, but I didn't have time to care. Rafta glared and screamed an Enochian war cry.

"I challenge you, Stimson," he yelled in English, his yellow eyes piercing into me. "You are no formidable enemy to me."

"Get out of the way, Stimson," I heard Devereaux scream.

"It is our way," the Enochian Prefect said.

Why the hell is he still here? I thought as I stared at Rafta. I knew that the Prefect had not been killed since I heard his voice, but I did not know what type of damage Rafta's blast created.

I ignored both Devereaux and the Enochian Prefect. At that moment, the only thing in the world that existed was Rafta. He had killed too many of my friends and associates. He had helped kidnap Denise's daughter, which almost resulted in her death. He had tried to bring about the total

231

destruction of my planet through his machinations, just as I had once tried to destroy his world. For once, my guilt over releasing the virus did not figure into my actions.

I glared back at Rafta. "Any time you're ready, you ugly, blue son of a bitch." With the last word, I used a roundhouse kick to his jaw, which sent the alien staggering backwards.

Rafta recovered quickly. He charged me as only an Enochian could charge: controlled, but quick as hell. He stopped inches from me and then bounded over my head with a leap, but not before delivering a blow to the right side of my head with his massive arm. I hit the ground, knowing that I could not take much of that type of punishment. I rolled to my knees and turned to where he should have come down. He was there. I saw a blue foot lash out and hit my left arm. I thought I would black out with the pain.

But somehow, I rose to my feet. Rafta had started his charge toward me again. I held my ground. He screamed the war cry again. Others later told me I gave a yell of my own, I'm sure out of frustration, anger, and grief. I took two steps forward, just as Rafta was about to stop and leap over me again. Before he could jump, I lashed out my right foot and brought him to the ground in the same manner I had downed Dingo at the Martinez house. The next few seconds seemed to take an eternity.

I watched as Rafta fell face-first toward the stage. I spotted the hump on his back that contained most of the nerve center in the Enochian neurological system. Rafta hit the stage and bounced hard. I knew that I would have to hit the hump with all of my strength to bust the bone and skin surrounding it. Rafta tried to get his feet underneath him to leap out of his precarious position. I yelled and jumped on his back, slamming my fist into the hump. I felt the bone give way and I felt the squishiness of his nerve endings. Rafta shuddered beneath me. I brought my hand up, covered in blue goo, and slammed it into the wound again. My fist disappeared up to the wrist. Rafta convulsed violently beneath me. And then he was still. I removed my hand and scrambled to my feet, trembling.

"That was a damn stupid thing to do," Devereaux said as he walked up to me. Others were making sure that Rafta was dead. I was unconcerned about the matter. My right fist had most of his nerve structure covering it. "Why the hell didn't you just get out of the way and let us shoot the damn thing?"

I shrugged and shook my head. "Where's Dingo?"

Devereaux pointed to an alien with his head embedded in a speaker. Dingo wasn't moving. "He timed his jump just right to take a majority of the blast that was aimed at the Enochian Prefect," Devereaux said.

Still ignoring the pain in my broken arm, I ran to where the Enochian lay. "Help me get him out of this thing," I yelled to anyone listening.

Devereaux and another officer ran to help me with Dingo. We pulled him out of the speaker and turned him over gingerly. I tried to tear off the white tunic, which had a burn mark in the middle of the chest. Someone produced a pair of scissors, cut it, and tore the tunic off for me, exposing the chest. I saw the hole of a burn right through the smiley face portion of his tattoo. I didn't know if it went all the way through him or not. Putting my head to his chest, I listened.

"Hey," I yelled, "get the paramedics. He's still breathing." I felt a tap on my shoulder.

"Sir, get out of my way and we'll get him to a hospital." I turned around to see the uniform of the New Orleans Fire Department.

"No, take him to my ship," I heard a deep Enochian voice say. "He will get the treatment he needs from Enochian doctors." That was true, I thought. I looked up to see the Enochian Prefect standing above me. "Though I believe he may be a hero. He deserves the honor."

I moved out of the way and let the paramedics strap him to a backboard. Two New Orleans police officers helped lift him and take him to the ambulance.

"Captain Stimson?" I turned around and looked up at the Prefect. "You truly are a formidable enemy and a formidable friend." I just looked at the Prefect and then turned to watch the ambulance pull away.

I saw Devereaux walk up to Boudreau. The senator turned red in the face and vehemently protested to the detective. I saw Devereaux grab Boudreau's shirt collar and pull him down to his level. Boudreau shut up and allowed police officers to handcuff him. Boudreau glared toward me.

I glared back. Somehow, I knew that Boudreau would be able to deny any involvement and would try to blame Gamble for his arrest. Still, I guessed that his presidential campaign was over for now.

Devereaux pushed Boudreau's head into the police car. I wanted to laugh, but I didn't have the strength. I felt weak and slightly dizzy. Another voice caught my attention as Boudreau was driven away.

"Mr. Stimson, I'm President Gamble." I turned to look at the man extending his hand toward me. "I'd just like to thank you—"

That was all I heard before I passed out. Devereaux told me later that I had thrown up on Gamble's shoes and fallen into his arms. I don't remember, but I kind of hoped he was right.

★ ★ ★ ★ ★

I woke up in the hospital with a splitting headache and the feeling that there were tubes in places where no tubes should ever be placed. I glanced around the room and realized that I was in the Intensive Care Unit. My eyes stopped on the woman who was slumped in a chair near my bed. She breathed as if she was asleep. I recognized Denise. A nurse walked into the room. I couldn't remember her name, but she had pulled a few shifts with me in the ER.

" 'Bout damn time you woke up," she said, smiling at me. "You gave us all a good scare, I can tell you, especially watching the fight."

"The fight?" I was surprised that she had seen it. "Were you there?"

She laughed. "Roger, the whole damn world was there. Some people say it was the most watched fight in the history of television."

I had not thought about the news channels being there. The whole thing had unfolded on live television. The nurse continued talking; I wished she would turn her nametag around.

"You're a big-shot hero now," she said. "But don't think that will get you any special treatment—"

Denise interrupted, speaking softly. "He could have been killed."

The nurse bent over the bed to straighten the covers, and whispered in my ear so that Denise couldn't hear. "She's been here all day waiting for you to wake up." She smoothed the blanket, seeming pleased with her work. She winked at me as she walked out.

I turned to Denise. "How's Kristen?"

"She's doing better than you at the moment," she said, raising an eyebrow. She stood and came closer to the bed.

"Just what did you think you were doing, fighting an Enochian warrior with only one arm?"

"It seemed like the thing to do at the moment." I tried to sit up and moaned, falling back onto the bed. "Concussion?" I asked. Denise nodded. "Any bleeds?"

"The doctor said the CT scan of your head didn't find anything out of the ordinary," she said, studying me. "I took that to mean that he couldn't find a brain, considering your actions this morning."

I looked around for a window. I knew there wasn't one, but I looked anyway. "What time is it?"

"It's eleven at night. That's why you're in the Intensive Care Unit, because you wouldn't wake up." She was silent for a moment. "I'm glad you did, though."

"Yeah, me too," I said, smiling at her. She smiled back and I felt a warm glow begin to infuse my body. Then I was reminded of the extra tubing I had acquired. I thought of another subject quickly. "Have you heard anything about Dingo?"

Her smile softened and, looking sad, she shook her head.

"Does that mean you haven't heard or—"

"I haven't heard," she said, quietly. "The last we saw of him, he was being loaded on the Enochian Prefect's shuttle. Detective Devereaux said the Enochians have been very closed-mouthed about Dingo since the shooting."

She smiled again. "But you're a hero, according to all the news commentators," she said, and then she laughed. "Only one of them said that you were crazy for fighting that alien alone."

We were silent for a while. Then Denise leaned down and kissed me tenderly on the lips. I gently grabbed the back of her neck as she started to straighten up, and pulled her face back to me and kissed her hard. I forgot my headache and almost forgot the damn tube. Well, I forgot it for about ten seconds.

She sat back down and we talked until about three. We'd let things settle down and figure out if our feelings were more than the adrenaline of the moment. I knew my answer, but I agreed.

After she left, I wondered about Dingo. Was he a hero after all? I hoped not. Life would be dull without Dingo.

30

A day after the assassination attempt, I lay in my hospital bed watching the news channels. When I saw my fight with Rafta, I had to agree with Denise that fighting an Enochian—and me with one broken arm—was not an intelligent thing to do. I got lucky. I was glad that the nurse had brought pain medication an hour before, when I saw the news conference start under a banner that read, "Breaking News."

The New Orleans Police Department had called the news conference, which would deal with the detainment of Senator Rafe Boudreau. Behind the red-faced Police Commissioner, I saw a smiling Rafe Boudreau and a dour-looking Detective Devereaux.

"I have a short statement," the Commissioner said, "and then I will turn the microphone over to Senator Boudreau. I will take no questions." He stared at the reporters as if daring them to say anything. Hundreds of cameras clicked and whirred. The background flashed with the photographers' bulbs. None of the reporters said a word, waiting for the Commissioner's statement.

"The City of New Orleans and the New Orleans Police Department would like to thank Senator Rafe Boudreau for his cooperation and understanding in our investigation of events that led up to the assassination attempt on President Gamble and the Enochian Prefect. We are emphatically denying that Senator Boudreau is now, or ever was, in our custody as anything other than a material witness." The

Commissioner looked up. "Thank you."

I shook my head. Boudreau had dodged another sticky situation by having deniability. Who would be his fall guy this time, since I wasn't available for the job? My money was on Lolich.

Boudreau stepped to the microphone. "I would like to thank the City and the Police Department for their actions in this matter. I understand why I was detained. Dennis Lolich had been in my employ, but I had no knowledge of his ties to the Sons of Earth and James Williams. I demanded and received Lolich's resignation from my staff, when I found out about the connection two weeks ago. I'll have a copy of his dated and signed resignation letter available for the public later this afternoon."

Reporters blitzed him with questions, which Boudreau answered in his glib, confident style. I was thankful that the pain medication began working, and was almost asleep when one reporter asked about me. "What can you tell me about Roger Stimson?"

Boudreau blinked. "I've known Roger Stimson for a long time. He is my friend, and I think we all owe him our gratitude and thanks."

I turned the television off and closed my eyes before I threw up. Boudreau told outright lies, and no one could prove anything different. Even though I could testify that Lolich was with the senator when they visited me a few days before, I could not prove it. The bastard was cheeky enough to call me a friend. Boudreau would walk away and probably become stronger than ever.

Hell, *he'd* turned himself into a *victim.*

A few days later, both Kristen and I had been released from the hospital and, at the insistence of the Enochian Prefect, we convalesced at Dingo's home. Besides, my apartment still contained a few too many openings in its walls. The Enochians would not acknowledge that Dingo existed, much less whether his wounds had been life-threatening.

No one could find out anything for me. Dingo disappeared into the Enochian Prefect's ship and no information was released about him. Devereaux inquired, as did the Secret Service agent, Michelle Allen, to no avail. The Enochians kept his condition and whereabouts secret. I concluded that Dingo had become an Enochian hero, which filled me with a sadness that surprised me because of its depth.

Staying at Dingo's kept me out of the limelight. In the days following the aborted assassination attempt, reporters had hounded me at the hospital. I answered their questions with a terse statement I released before disappearing: "Roger Stimson is a private citizen and intends to remain a private citizen. He will answer no questions nor give any interviews to the press." Devereaux had helped me get away without being seen. And no one knew where Dingo had lived, since the house was owned by numerous dummy corporations the Enochian had set up when he was a "Trade Liaison" of the Enochian Prefect.

Trade Liaison. Right.

Denise and Kristen had left earlier that day for their trip back to Midland. We cried in each other's arms, but we both knew it was best for the moment. I knew that I would see her again. I hoped she would feel the same. We needed time to sort out what was real emotion and what was the kind of emotional bonding that took place in stressful situations. Besides, Denise's first job was the care and recovery of Kristen.

I sat in a chair feeling melancholy, staring at the desk

where I had seen Dingo trying to break into the Secret Service computer network. When the phone rang, I jumped and stared at it until it rang again. Few people knew where I was staying, so I was wary about answering the phone.

"Hello," I said cautiously.

"Stimson, it's Devereaux."

"Hi, Detective," I said. "I see you survived the incident with Boudreau."

"Yeah, well, he couldn't say too much," Devereaux said. "His former bodyguard was definitely involved, so he had to thank us and praise us. Did a right good job of portraying himself as a victim, didn't he?"

" 'Former bodyguard,' my ass. Boudreau planned this operation. I know it, and so do you."

I heard Devereaux sigh. "Doesn't matter now. The only person who could implicate him just floated up from the bottom of one the canals with his two bodyguards." He paused to let the news sink in. I said nothing.

"We just received confirmation that one of the bodies was that of James Williams, head of the Sons of Earth," Devereaux said. "All three had gunshot wounds to the head. Ballistics matched the bullets to Lolich's weapon. Just thought you ought to know."

"Thanks, Detective." I hung up and stared at a wall for a long while, wondering if I should find Boudreau and take my own vengeance. I shook my head and realized it was getting late.

As I was just getting up to fix a bit of dinner, the doorbell rang. I looked through the peephole and saw a mailman waiting for me to answer.

"Yeah, what do you want?"

"Got a certified letter," he said cheerfully. "You need to sign for it." I opened the door and signed for the letter. He turned away and walked off.

I closed the door and returned to the living room, opening the envelope. I was stunned when I saw what it contained. The Enochians had sent me the fully paid deed to the house. I took it as confirmation that Dingo was dead. He had become a hero, after all. Of course, I couldn't accept the gift, but I wasn't sure that I could give it back without insulting the Enochians. I shrugged and put the deed on the coffee table. I could deal with this when things settled down.

I turned on the radio as I walked into the kitchen. A familiar tune was playing, and I found myself humming along. I shook my head, realizing that someone had jumped on the Dingo bandwagon. He had been declared a hero on Earth, dead or alive, for his actions last Monday. I sang the chorus with the singer, tears forming in my eyes. I felt an odd camaraderie with the dead Enochian. We had both done what we felt like we had to do.

"D-I-N-G-O and Dingo was his name-O."

ABOUT THE AUTHOR

TERRY BRAMLETT writes speculative fiction from the comfort of his Mississippi home, which he shares with his wife Brenda and the obligatory animals he acquired when he started writing. He has sold short stories to *Weird Tales*, *Oceans of the Mind*, *H.P. Lovecraft's Magazine of Horror*, *Neo-Opsis*, and various other magazines. *Formidable Enemy* is his first novel.